This edition first published 2019 by Fahrenheit Thirteen, an imprint of Fahrenheit Press.

ISBN: 978-1-912526-59-8

10 9 8 7 6 5 4 3 2 1

www.Fahrenheit-Press.com

F 4 E

Dead Cat Bounce

By

Robert White

Fahrenheit Thirteen

An Imprint of Fahrenheit Press

For Tom Huff

CHAPTER 1

Old Mrs. Bello lived upstairs from the family grocery store all her life. Her grandfather had settled in Brockton at the same time as the Maronis came over on the same boat. Mrs. Bello kept his ticket for passage in steerage in one of the shoe boxes where she kept all her money. She didn't trust banks. Many old Italian families who'd gone through the bleak years of the Depression did the same thing; they stuffed money under mattresses or in Mason jars. It wasn't uncommon for that generation of Italian-Americans who never spoke English and never stepped outside their community. What was different in her case was that she never changed, despite the husband and four kids, and later, the seven grandkids, and when she died at 88 years of age, all $262,998 was in seventeen shoe boxes stacked one on top of the other, exactly where she left it.

Her husband Carmine predeceased her in 1996. By the time she died in 2004, following a fall and a short stay in a nursing home, her children and grandchildren were all living in other cities or other states. Giovanni, the eldest, was the first to leave "Taxachusetts," as he and his siblings mockingly referred to their natal state. He had a modest but successful dental practice in Providence. Cynthia, being the youngest, was the last to leave home; she married her high-school boyfriend who'd impregnated her in sophomore year. In those days, the nuns would have tarred-and-feathered any girl who got pregnant and thought she'd remain in school. "Bold as brass" was still a favorite family saying resulting from years of parochial education by the Sisters of the Holy Humility of Mary. Cindy spent her maternity months living with an aunt in Taunton. All Mrs. Bello's children did reasonably well by middle-class standards. None achieved extraordinary prosperity, however, which was one reason why every one of the Bello children was upset that no money was found after their mother's death.

A day didn't pass when a cell-phone conversation with one or the other didn't occur among them. Where did it go? was the question asked of one another a hundred times. No one knew where and no one knew exactly how much their mother had squirreled away out of her phobia regarding banks and bankers. As children growing up, the store was on its last legs, but their father had a good job on the railroad and he dutifully gave his wife every dime of his paychecks for the forty-five years of their (more or less) happy marriage.

The old building was an eyesore with loose bricks falling to the sidewalk and broken glass or planking over the upstairs windows. Siding had been stripped off by addicts as high as they could reach and sold to junkyards. Vandals had long ago smashed the big front plate-glass windows where Mrs. Bello and Carmine used to display various food items for sale that day or week. On one of his holidays from grad school, John had removed the last shards of glass and nailed plywood over the gaping holes.

Fewer than a dozen of the old Italian families were left to cling to the neighborhood by the time the children were grown and gone. The textile industry that once gave so many good-paying jobs was barely a memory to Brockton's youth. Drugs and gangs had taken over Mrs. Bello's neighborhood and scrawled their graffiti on every deserted factory building or abandoned storefront like hers. It almost tore the family apart when they finally agreed to sell the building. For a brief time, a boxing promoter had rented the building and invited neighborhood youth to work out on the premises. He put an ad in the paper and painted the front of the building in splashy Caribbean colors. Inspired by native sons Rocky Marciano's and "Marvelous" Marvin Hagler's illustrious careers in fisticuffs, he'd hoped to become the next Emanuel Steward and make the converted storefront a gym famous enough to rival Detroit's Kronk. It was not to be. Though well-intentioned, his effort was too little, too late. Boxing was no longer seen as a way out of the ghetto. Neighborhood kids wore Celtics or Tom Brady jerseys, Red Sox ball caps (backwards in the de rigeuer style of the day). Basketball was the preferred alternative and didn't leave you reeling from CTE at the end of your sports career. On top of that, rap and hip-hop were far more attractive and lucrative. Every teenager wanted to be the next Beyoncé or the next Bruno Mars.

Throughout the years and decades of decay, neighborhood rumors persisted that money was hidden in the house. Certainly, the family believed it. They'd shared the cost of taxes when no one offered to take it on and agreed beforehand any money found would be split evenly. They also agreed not to search the premises alone—there had to be at least two other siblings accompanying the searcher. Each one had logged hours in separate dawn-to-dusk searches and come out empty with faces blackened from removing wall paneling, climbing among the pipework and tearing apart ducts to search inside. The refrigerator, of course, was opened and shut a thousand times. But not once did anyone think to pull it away from the wall to look behind it. Even though it was an old-fashioned model from the 1970s that even short-statured Carmine could have looked over the top of on his tip-toes, the siblings knew their old overweight mother, wheezing from shortness of breath and wrapped in her familiar black shawl like some ancient Strega Nona, could never have pushed it away from the wall with her arthritic joints and bad knees.

CHAPTER 2

The day Butchie Parmenter found the money, he was inside the place on legitimate business. He'd used his father's position as sergeant-at-arms with the Christopher Columbus Lodge to pull enough strings to get him hired on with the city as a housing inspector. For Butchie, this was locking a kid with a sweet tooth inside a candy store; he was a thief. Being free to walk into houses was his dream job. He scoped out empty houses during work hours and came back in the evenings to rip out copper pipes and tubing. Trouble was, the junkies didn't leave much. But anything of value, anything worth fencing, went into the back of his Ford F-150, a rusted-out junker, under a blue plastic tarpaulin. His new Jeep Wrangler sat out front of his apartment in his allotted space; it was too obvious to take on his off-duty "excursions." He even drove to the municipal parking lot with stolen goods still tied down in the back.

There was an unexpected bonus to Butchie's job: he encountered some single mothers who weren't repulsed by his flirting and a few more than willing to supplement their welfare checks with a quick romp in a bedroom while their toddler watched cartoons. He'd gotten good at sensing which women were amenable to his charms and which were merely polite from those who'd report him in a heartbeat. Butchie loved the challenge. Taking bribes from landlords who failed inspections was the other side of that coin. All in all, he felt himself a lucky man—that is, until the day he found the shoeboxes stuffed with tens, twenties, and fifties in the Bello building.

The city had planned to tear it down, but the family engaged a lawyer to halt the proceedings. The filing of writs by both sides resulted in a declaration of lis pendens in which the court assumed control over the building until the matter could be formally settled. Butchie was there to ascertain the current status of the building as a fire or pedestrian hazard.

Butchie had just come from the building after one of his cursory inspections and was killing time in a bar on Main with Nino Frabutt when Odraye Suggs walked in. Nino called Suggs over to their booth and introduced him to Butchie.

"Odraye here's a boxer," Nino said. "Come sit down, champ."

Suggs barely placed his hand in Butchie's and avoided giving a squeeze, which irked Butchie. Man thinks his hand's a Fabergé egg.

"That so?" Butchie said. "You fight anybody I know?"

Odraye named three fighters with whom he'd had bouts in club fights around Massachusetts, all heavyweights like him, but omitted the fact (Butchie looked him up later) that all three out of eight career fights were losses, two technical KOs and a split decision.

"They call him 'The Wild Panamanian,'" Nino said. "He likes to head-butt."

"Fuck you, Nino," Odraye said.

"You from Panama?" Butchie asked. Like most Caucasians, he didn't distinguish mixed races easily, and Odraye's features appeared altogether African-American.

Nino laughed.

"What is it? Did I say something funny?" Butchie asked Nino.

"Yeah, he's Panamanian, all right," Nino said. "Panama City, Florida. The 'Wild' part comes from his head-butting. How many fights got you disqualified, Odraye?"

Odraye raised three fingers and slowly lowered all but the middle one, which he aimed at Nino. All three laughed.

Nino knocked back the last of his beer and stood up. "Look, I gotta run, fellas," he said. "I'll see youse later."

"You know Nino a long time?" Butchie asked Odraye.

"We went to Brockton High, same class," he replied.

"Me too," Butchie said. "Cheers, man."

He lifted his glass in a toast. Butchie didn't mention he'd dropped out at sixteen with a forged signature from his mother, well into early onset dementia at that point. He'd finished his GED solely to land a job with the city or the county, a basic requirement, and that thanks to his mother's brother.

Odraye said he worked for an air-conditioning company on Montello and asked Butchie if he lived in the area.

"No, I've got an apartment on Belmont," he said. "I'm just coming from a job."

Butchie mentioned the old Bello place and Odraye leaned across the table.

"Man, you know there's a fortune in cash hidden in that shithole somewhere. People been lookin' for it for years."

"What do you mean?"

Odraye gave him a summary of the neighborhood gossip regarding the old woman and her missing fortune "stuffed up a chimney" or "tucked behind a wall somewhere."

"You are shitting me," Butchie said.

"Hell, no, man, I am not shitting you. I trained in there for a while when it was a gym."

Odraye told him he heard about it from the guy who ran the gym and operated as a matchmaker for his bouts. They'd scoured every inch of the building together, agreeing to a 50-50 split.

"Ain't no damn money in there," Odraye said. "Else we'd a found it."

"Maybe not," Butchie said.

Odraye leaned across the table again. Butchie noticed he had big boxer's hands with white points on the knuckles, the "diamond points" of macho boxers who liked to hit the bags bare-handed but affected a delicate handshake like a debutante.

Butchie had already sized up Odraye as a liar and con artist.

He's big, looks dangerous like he's waiting for the chance to cadge a few bucks off me but sly enough not to threaten, lets his size do the talking. Butchie prided himself on his street smarts. He knew how to spot a hustler.

"Look," he said. "The city's gonna tear that building down real soon, maybe a couple months at the most. If there is money in there—"

"No doubt about it, homes," Odraye interjected. "There is money in there. Every fool around here knows that old lady died with all her cash left in there somewhere—just waitin' for somebody to walk in and pick it up!"

"—if there is money hidden in that place, I can get us the tools and the permits to start demolishing it without anybody being the wiser."

"Fifty-fifty," Odraye said.

"Fifty-fifty, you got it, bro," Butchie said. He leaned back in the booth and smiled, thinking he had nothing to lose, and if he did find anything, it might be worth his while to distract Odraye while he figured out a better hiding spot until he could get it all. Why not? You got to risk it to get the biscuit—one of his old man's favorite sayings, although his three years in Plymouth for check forgery might not be the best testament to that aphorism.

CHAPTER 3

"Nino, it's me, Butchie."

"Yo, Butchie, what up?"

"Odraye Suggs. What can you tell me about him?"

"Like I said, he's a good dude."

"Can I trust him?"

"Well, yeah, like, I mean he bullshits about his record, but ya know, every fighter does that. Ain't been back in the ring since he took that fight with what's-his-name, some tomato can from Boston he shoulda beat and got hit with so many punches it looked like a glove factory fell in on him."

"I don't care about boxing, Nino. I wanna to know if he's straight. Can I trust him?"

"You can trust The Panamanian. He ain't the sharpest stick in the forest, but you can trust him."

"Bye."

Butchie had the tools and an orange city work permit he'd Xeroxed at work for tacking to the door. A little doctoring and it looked legit. Might not fool a cop but any curious locals popping their heads in to see what was going on inside would see the permit. This was a gamble, Butchie knew, because it meant his cushy job with the city if anything broke bad on the caper. He had people at work giving him side-eye looks as it was, and he had a bigger worry just then.

Delores Negrón, to give that particular worry a name, was high on something when he came calling for a house inspection last week. She was renting from some shitbird ex-con named Quinnel Jones, who'd found Jesus in prison and was getting his life back together by way of remodeling his mother's house on Centre Street. He already had a tenant although the place wasn't up to code yet. Butchie was dropping by and he'd explain things to Quinnel, how it worked and so forth. Most landlords paid up on the spot and were grateful to Butchie for not reporting them. Every now and then a landlord would balk, and he'd walk back his invitation to square things up without "the city getting its nose into the guy's private business." It always came down to Butchie's word against a slumlord.

Delores, the tenant, said Quinnel had to run an errand and he'd be right there. She was wearing a shorty nightgown, all frills and tiny bows, and a lot of cleavage on display; she'd coyly pretend to tuck herself back in whenever she leaned over. She knew what she was doing and Butchie figured, why not? He'd fallen into a honeytrap before, right after he broke up with Denise. That one left a message on his voicemail about "needing some cash for some Pampers and milk." Butchie didn't see any babies in the place, and even if she did have kids, he should have suspected a shakedown coming when Quinnel didn't show after fifteen minutes, and the woman was doing a slow strip tease in front of him. Stupid, I should have seen this coming.

But right at the moment, the more pressing concern was getting inside the old store and tearing the place apart. He had mattocks, crowbars, drills and circular saws, along with sledgehammers and LED lantern lights he bought from a TV ad. He told Odraye they'd do all the drywall tonight.

"You mean we ain't gonna look around first?" Odraye asked.

"Well, if we saw a garbage bag stuffed with cash, sure, we'll pick it up off the floor. That'll save some time."

"I mean, you know," Odraye said, stifling his anger at the wisecrack, "what if she had a favorite hiding spot in the bedroom. That's where we should go first."

"Whatever, man," Butchie said, "just be ready at six-fifteen. I'll be out front in the truck waiting."

Odraye was standing out front of his apartment complex

on Commercial Street when Butchie rolled up.

"You look spiffy, Odraye," he said.

"What's that mean?"

"Something my old man used to say. You ready to tear her up tonight—get that green?"

"You just stay clear when I'm swinging one of them sledgehammers you got in the back," Odraye said.

Butchie kept the friendly grin pasted on his face, but Odraye's tone implied he'd just made a Freudian slip, or some kind of unconscious slip, because Butchie had the same instincts about not turning his back on Odraye—just in case that money was lying around in plain sight in a garbage bag. One Norwegian rat silently communicating to the other, and no matter what Nino said about trusting Odraye, he damn sure wasn't going to turn his back on the pug with a sledgehammer in his hands and a bag of money to be split 50-50.

They hadn't gone ten minutes before Odraye said, "We might have a problem."

"What do you mean, we might have a problem?"

Odraye shifted against the seat back and said, "There's a dude, lives nearby. He saw me scoping the place this afternoon—"

"Jesus Christ, I told you not to go near it until we had the permit."

"Yeah, yeah, man, I know, I know."

"You know."

"But, like, damn, that Leotis, he's all over me. He sees me when I come out—"

"You were in there?"

Butchie almost choked on the words.

"Shit, man, everybody's been inside that place! Got gang graffiti all over the walls—"

"Odraye."

"—like, squatters been in there. Practically a needle palace at night with all the junkies comin' and goin'"

"Odraye."

"What?"

"Nothing."

Butchie had to unclench his jaws to keep his teeth from biting through his lips.

"Oh hell, there he is," Odraye said.

A tall gangly black male with a hunch was standing on the corner in front of the store.

"I take it that's Leotis," Butchie said.

"Leotis Marsten, Jr. He's OK, though. He ain't interested in no money."

Butchie bit back his first response and asked, as calmly as he could manage, "How do you know?"

"He told me, man. He just wants the damn refrigerator for his moms. He said he'd give me ten if I helped him tote it out of there."

Leotis waved to Odraye as Butchie pulled around the corner. They'd have to lug the tools to the front door but that was all right. He didn't want to make it too conspicuous for any cops cruising past, and in a high-crime neighborhood like this one, they were never far away.

Butchie slammed the gear shift into park and said, "You want to be seen looting a refrigerator out of that place when there could be a fortune inside? You really think that's wise, Odraye?"

"It's how we gonna get rid of him, man. I told you. He'll hang around all night until he gets that thing."

"OK," Butchie said, swallowing hard. "How far does it have to go."

"Just across the street. You see that brick house? That's his momma's hair-styling business."

"Let's do it first thing, fast as we can," Butchie said.

Butchie jimmied the hasp on the padlock with too much force; the wood was dry-rotted, and the hasp flew off. Leotis fetched it and followed them inside.

"What a dump," Odraye said. "Smells like a toilet."

"It was someone's home once," Butchie said, wondering why he felt a pang of nostalgia for it.

They wandered in a slow zig-zag taking in the spacious rooms, the graffiti, the molding in the corners. The kitchen was the last room at the back. A single window was all there was to let in light.

"There she is. I'll help you boys," Leotis said.

Butchie smiled at him. Odraye hadn't bothered to introduce him.

"No, that's fine. We'll handle it. You just lead the way."

"You got a dolly for it?"

"Darn, I must have left it back at the garage. We'll just have to carry it ourselves, me and this big guy here. He can probably carry it all by himself."

"Kiss my ass."

Leotis laughed. "Odraye here worries about CTE, like all them football players. That's why he don't fight no more. Boxers, she-yit, all you guys probably got it!" He did an Ali pantomime with shaking hands.

"Leotis, I'll knock you out right here and then you can tell me all about CTE."

"OK, OK, man, be cool. I'm just havin' some fun wit' you."

"Odraye, I suggest you tilt it toward you and we get this man's mother this refrigerator before the rest of the neighborhood comes by for some lamps and that old sofa back there."

"Oh no, man, you don't want to take that," Leotis said. "It's nasty. Some white skank was doin' tricks on it to pay for her blast. They had a line goin' out the door for her last night wrapped clear around the corner."

Butchie squeezed his eyes shut and silently counted to three before he spoke. "Odraye, I would like to get to work. We're on city time here, remember? Let's shove it away from the wall first and then you tilt it toward me."

A plastic grill over the motor popped loose as they shimmied it back and forth to gain momentum. It came away from the wall a few feet easily enough and then Odraye rocked it to a twenty-degree angle, holding it by his fingertips from the top. A clattering sound came from behind it.

"What's that?"

"Tilt it back upright," Butchie said.

Leotis slipped a hand behind the refrigerator and came away with a shoebox. It was taped shut with masking tape, the tape had turned yellow like the color of the yellow sticky fly strips still dangling from the ceiling fan overhead.

Butchie and Odraye stared at each other.

Leotis ripped the lid off with his fingertips. "What's this? What the hell's—Oh my God!"

"The goddamned refrigerator," Butchie said in a voice more a whisper. "Who'd have believed it? Nobody bothered to look behind the frigging refrigerator all these years? There it was, all this time—"

Odraye's right fist lashed out and took Leotis on the left side of the jaw. He crumpled to the floor unconscious; the box of money flew out of his hands and thick wads of bills spilled out, all rolled tight and secured with rubber bands.

Butchie looked at Odraye again. The whites of his eyes were marbled with veins like tiny forks of lightning.

Odraye said nothing; he rubbed his knuckles against his work coveralls. He stepped back where the two sledgehammers were leaning against the wall. Without taking his eyes off Butchie for a second, he reached down and grabbed the nearest handle and brought it to his side.

Butchie hadn't been in a street fight since eighth-grade when he was a crossing guard for Our Lady of Sorrows and a taller black kid from the public school challenged him to fight for no reason. With two classmates looking on, he had no choice. The fight didn't last long and Butchie's face was smeared with blood from accurate jabs to the nose. Butchie laughed about it later. "I bled all over him," he said on the playground, but getting hit in the face and being unable to do anything about it was the most powerless feeling he had ever experienced.

"Why did you do that?"

"I think you know," Odraye said. "I think you know, Butchie."

Leotis twitched on the floor and his eyelids fluttered, but he was out.

Odraye's size and speed became a singular blur, impossible to focus, but that lizard brain in Butchie's head told him to duck. Instinctively, he raised his arms across his face to ward off the coming blow and propelled himself backwards to the floor.

It never came. His next sensation was the sound of bone shattering like a pumpkin dropped on pavement. More like flung down from over the head. The meat end of the sledgehammer was sunk into Leotis's head nearly to the shaft.

Scrambling to his feet, adrenalin nearly gagging him, Butchie looked at the damage. His face felt on fire and every hair on his body was standing at attention.

"Oh my Jesus Christ, Odraye!"

Leotis twitched on the floor, a belated muscle spasm of nerves receiving a message from the brain but the citadel had been abandoned. Odraye twisted the steel head out of Leotis's skull; blood dripped into the gaping hole.

"Christ, Christ, Christ—"

"Your turn," Odraye said; he thrust the handle hard against Butchie's chest. "Hit him."

"Mother of God, Odraye, he's dead!"

"I know it, but you got to do it. We in this together, remember?"

"I can't—"

"Do it!"

The menace in Odraye's voice was chilling enough but the subtext of the message was clear: hit him or it comes down on your head next.

Butchie allotted a full second to the alternative: he could attack Odraye, use the hammer, try to get out of the place without being killed by the bigger man. When that second elapsed, he knew it was hopeless; he was a coward. Odraye would take that hammer away from him and use his head for a croquet ball before Butchie could lift it in his direction.

He looked down at Leotis's corpse. He noticed the legs of

his coveralls were spattered with blood spray from the force of Odraye's swing. Butchie lifted the sledge to his shoulder and let the head drop down into the messy crater of Leotis's head.

"There, you got his blood on you, too," Odraye said. "Fifty-fifty."

Odraye snatched the handle from Butchie's grip. The two men stared at each other.

"What now?" Butchie asked.

"Watch him," Odraye said. "I'll be right back."

Butchie's knees felt as if he'd been tapped with a tine hammer; the adrenalin jolt was still coursing through his bloodstream. He didn't dare to show weakness. In truth, the animal part of him was throwing a celebration party he was still alive, and he hadn't joined Leotis down on that dusty floor. Odraye had to be thinking about killing him, too, assessing the odds. Butchie looked at the blood pooling around Leotis's head, a garish halo, now oblong as gravity changed the flow in one direction.

Butchie heard the clomp of Odraye's boot steps coming down. He realized he hadn't heard him go upstairs.

"I found a place," he said.

All the rooms upstairs were used for smoking or shooting dope. Discarded needles littered the floor, old paper bags that once held forties were left to disintegrate like the empty bags of chips and Cheeto's dropped by the weed smokers to satisfy hunger jags. One room must have been used by the boozers; old vodka and whiskey bottles lay strewn around the threadbare carpeting with fleur-de-lis designs. Sun-rotted sheers flapped in the open windows. The stench of rodent urine was more powerful in this room.

They lay Leotis against a wall and rammed an ancient velour sofa up against his body.

He'd carried the feet while Odraye had him under the arms, a lantern resting on the dead man's stomach to negotiate the narrow stairs from the kitchen to the upper floors. Butchie felt a moment of giddy hysteria pass through him as light bounced off the crushed remains of Leotis Marsten's head. A twenty-gauge with buckshot would have done similar damage.

They returned downstairs, Butchie held the walls with the palms of his hands to keep his legs from wobbling. Odraye led the way.

They counted the shoeboxes; each one packed with money—not just ones but big bills. A couple were wrapped with fifties. The currency was old. Abe and George didn't have such big heads. Butchie unwrapped one wad and saw a dozen bills with orange stamping and a portrait he didn't recognize in the dim lighting. He put the bill under one of the lantern lights: McKinley, a smooth-shaved President, on a bill he had never seen before: 500.

Together they scooped up the boxes and cradled them against their chest to make one trip.

"This is crazy," Butchie hollered to him. "They'll see us leaving with these."

Nothing deterred Odraye. He bulled through the door with the swag without bothering to look back. Butchie wondered, hoped even, he'd keep going; instead, he threw the boxes into the back of the truck and got in and sat there.

You just murdered a man and he's sitting there like a cigar-store Indian, Butchie thought.

Butchie threw his load into the back, flipped the tarp over everything and secured it with bungee cord.

"We've got to go back inside," he told Odraye.

"What for? Let's get the fuck out of here right now."

"The sledge, for one thing," Butchie said. "Got our prints all over it."

He ran back inside, convinced a dozen pairs of eyes were boring into him. His heart was beating like a hummingbird's. He scuffed up the kitchen floor as best he could, erasing their boot prints, tossing trash around. The refrigerator had to be shoved back against the wall, and he called Odraye over to help him. At the last second, he remembered the sledgehammer and picked it up. The thought of Odraye having it in his hands sent an icy chill up his spine. If he wanted to leave the crime scene without bothering to clean up, he'd have no qualms about bashing in Odraye's brains too and leaving him on the floor.

The fridge replaced, they wiped it down with some rags from the bed of the pickup.

"What else did you touch?"

"Fuck if I know," Odraye said. "C'mon, let's go, Butchie."

What was that shit on those crime shows—the one he liked, where they talked about "fracture matches" on duct tape and "transfer fibers"? Oh Lord, Leotis was probably covered with them, but he had no stomach to go back upstairs. The image of the dead man was already seared into his brain.

"Let's go, God damn it!"

The last thing to be removed was the fake work permit; Butchie snatched it from the door and headed around to the driver's side. A dark SUV passed him as he bent low to the door to keep his face hidden from view of the driver.

"Slow down—slow the fuck down!"

Butchie eased his foot from the gas. He was speeding, unconsciously escaping that horror show behind him. His brain pinwheeled despite his effort to focus on the road.

"How much?"

"How. . . much?"

"Yeah, man, how much money you think we got back there?"

"I don't know," Butchie replied. "I don't know."

"A couple hundred thousand, easy," Odraye said.

"I've got to pull over," Butchie said.

"Wh—what?"

He swung the ford into the curb, scraping the tires. He popped the door and leaned over just as a spume of vomit ejected from his stomach.

A powerful hand on Butchie's collar snapped him back into the driver's position. Butchie put his hand to his mouth to catch the next stream but his fingers had the same effect as gripping a hose and his vomit sprayed in all directions—hitting the windshield, the side window, the steering wheel, and Odraye's shoulder.

"You motherfucker—"

Butchie held his hand up. "I'm OK, I'm OK, I'm OK—"

Then a third and final volley of his stomach contents blew over the same areas as before. Butchie's head throbbed from the retching and he turned a sickly grin toward Odraye. Odraye was trying to flick vomit off his chin and staring at his fingertips. Before Butchie could apologize, Odraye's fist snapped out in a short, hard jab to his jaw.

Before a shimmering red curtain came down over his eyes, he remembered being in church, St. John Boscoe's at high mass during Christmas. He and his big sister were kneeling in the pew when Butchie felt lightheaded from the flu and the fact he couldn't keep food down. He tipped over backwards, slamming his head on the pew's curved arm rest, in the process embarrassing his older sister Maeve, who wouldn't let him forget it afterward. Down, down into the comforting dark was—as he would remember it later on—a mighty relief from the inner turbulence left behind.

A last screenshot in the neocortex, of Nino in the bar: Yeah, you can trust him. . .

CHAPTER 4

"I thought for a minute there I was gonna have to call Nine-One-One."

"Jesus, my jaw," Butchie said, leaning up, groaning.

"My bad, man," Odraye said. "You sprayin' puke like it come out of a firehose. Got some of that shit on my new hoodie."

"Where's the money?"

Butchie looked around the cab, snapping to full alert.

"It's still in the back, where you think? C'mon, man, we need to go before some cop checks out why we stopped here."

"OK."

"Can you drive?"

"I can drive."

"Then let's go on and git, dog. We got to go count that money!"

Odraye's wide brown face beamed at him. For a man his size his teeth were small like a baby's, a feature which enhanced rather than lessened the menace. To Butchie, it resembled a giant baby with stomach gas; the smile was about as sincere.

Two-hundred-sixty-two-thousand, nine-hundred, ninety-eight dollars. It sat there in stacks of separate denominations. The pile of blue and red rubber bands that for decades had held the money in tight wads lay underfoot beneath the small table Butchie had hauled out to the garage. Only a few of the frayed rubber bands had held their elasticity. The money was a far cry from crisp; it had been a long time since it rolled off in sheets at the Bureau of Engraving. It seemed that old Mrs. Bello kept every dollar and only rarely traded up for bigger bills just to keep the ones from overflowing. She must have relaxed her phobia about banks in her old age, too, because not many Italians from those days in this working-class neighborhood walked around with twenties and fifties in their wallets.

"We got us a slight problem," Butchie said.

"What problem?"

"These bills, the printing, they're all outdated. Look at the size of Jackson's head. He looks like somebody shrunk it compared to the new ones."

"So what? It'll spend the same. Is—wait a minute. You sayin' this money won't spend?"

"It'll spend, all right. Kind of. The government has to redeem all banknotes at face value."

"Then cut me out my share of the good ones. You can worry about the other ones."

"Sure," Butchie said. "I'll do that but you gotta give me a percentage for my trouble."

Odraye shrugged his big shoulders and leaned across the table. His face scrunched up. Butchie could imagine his fighter's face in a staredown at his opponent while the referee's voice droned out the rules to both fighters.

"I don't want to wait," Odraye said. "I need the cash right now, you hearing me?"

"I'm saying," Butchie began, thinking he needed to be careful with his words, "that if we walk into a bank and ask for bills of the same value, we're likely to be remembered. Next thing you know, a couple dozen SWAT and two or three men in blue windbreakers with FBI letters on the back are thumping on the door at five in the morning."

"That's why we got to cut the money and split," Odraye said, "before some dope fiend lights up in that upstairs room and starts wonderin' if some rat died behind that red sofa."

"I don't think it'll take that long," Butchie said. "He was supposed to be delivering a refrigerator across the street, remember? How long do think it'll be before his mother reports him missing?"

"She ain't likely to say where he was," Odraye said. "I know that woman. She's an obituary liar. Nobody gonna believe her no matter what she says."

Obituary liar, habitual liar. . . Butchie rubbed his jaw and wondered if he should just turn himself in now, turn state's evidence, take whatever deal they offered, plead, and do the time. Murder meant Walpole, however. That was a serious place. Ex-cons who'd done time in Cedar Junction talked about Block 10. He knew he wasn't tough enough to stand up to it, and the thought of wearing a dress for some lifer and having his name changed to Mary wasn't how he wanted to spend the next ten to fifteen years.

Trouble was, Odraye glaring at him, clenching and unclenching his big fists across the table, wasn't helping him focus.

"Odraye, bro, look. We're in this together, right? We're joined at the hip because of. . . what went down back there. We got to make sure both of us stay safe."

"I don't think so, Butchie. I say we split the money right now. I'll take my chances. You go your way and I go mine. Simple."

Butchie suppressed a groan. Why hadn't he thought this out?

Odraye wasn't the same guy who had sat across from him in Shenanigan's and joked about his losses in the ring. He looked mean and all that damn money sorted by denomination and stacked like rows of cadets was pulling Odraye like a magnet toward certain disaster. Butchie had to make him see it or they both might as well turn themselves in.

"I understand what you're saying, Odraye. I do. But I need you to look at this my way for just a moment, OK? The money's right here. We're safe—for now. But we're gonna be our own worst enemies"—damn, wrong word—"if we don't act together."

Butchie interlaced his fingers and hit his chest with his

thumbs. Maybe a little visual aid would help make the point.

"What are you sayin'?"

"I'm saying we have to act normal," Butchie pleaded. "We go about our routines like nothing is different. We wait a week—"

"Fuck that."

"—we wait a couple days—just a couple days at most! Then we see how the land lies, so to speak. We find a way to exchange the money for new bills or deposit it in a bank where the management isn't going to have a shitfit when they see the amount we're bringing in, see? The feds got this law that says anybody depositing more than ten thousand gets reported to—the National Bank Authority."

"So what?"

"It's in case it's dope money," Butchie said, still winging it. "They got another law that says they are required to confiscate the cash right on the spot."

"Why not contact some of your goombahs in Boston, see will they take it all. We knock down the price, say, take seventy-, eighty cents on the dollar," Odraye said.

"My name's Parmenter, not Patriarca," Butchie said. "Odraye, I'm shocked. You assume because I'm Italian I must be connected to a crime family. That's racial profiling."

"No, it ain't, man. Getting pulled over for DWB, Driving While Black. That's racial profiling. I want my cut. I'll worry about passing the money myself."

Butchie hit panic mode. The thought of those bills on the street meant game over.

"You can't do that, man. These, these piles of money, they might as well be made of cigarette paper. Look, feel them! They got no colored inks, none of them security gizmos, the metal strips. You think you're gonna walk into a Duke and Duchess, buy a pack of cigarettes and hand the clerk this old-style twenty, and you're gonna get change back?"

"Why not just take the whole got-damn load to the bank? Tell 'em we want new money."

"Oh, you mean, your generous Aunt Lucille the rich

hoarder with varicose veins up and died and left you with all this money?"

"I ain't got no Aunt Lucille but what I do got is a right to half this cash," Odraye said and slammed his fist on the table hard enough to make all the stacks of bills levitate, a few bigger ones collapsing.

"I was using a figure of speech, Odraye," Butchie said. He kept his tone even. It was like having a grizzly opposite him, glaring, and a bunch of flopping salmon on the table. But he didn't know how to remove the distraction without drawing the bear's ire.

"OK, I agree with you—that's exactly what I'm talking about," Butchie said, ad-libbing wildly, before Odraye realized he didn't need his or anybody's permission.

Odraye suddenly leaned back in the chair, the wood squealing as his weight stressed the joints.

"I'm listening," he said.

"We exchange the money," Butchie said, picking up the thread, grateful for the pause. "All of it, one time. But we do it so we get away with it and we for shit-sure don't do it at any bank in Brockton."

"Why the hell not?"

"You told me yourself the day I met you," Butchie said. "You said everybody in the neighborhood knows old Mrs. Bello kept money in the house. They'll know. We have to have an airtight story."

Odraye said nothing. Butchie slowly exhaled; the danger had passed. He was sure for one long moment Odraye would rear up from that chair and scoop up his share of the cash—maybe a little more, as he knew Butchie wouldn't do anything about it. Then he'd leave. Butchie would start the doomsday clock from that second, figured he'd have maybe a week at most before the cops wrapped them both up.

With more eloquence than he'd ever been able to summon in his life, Butchie convinced Odraye they had to leave the money intact for the time being. Yes, counted and divided, two tall kitchen bags apiece. He pulled down the ladder to the garage loft and showed Odraye where the money would be hidden.

"That pink shit ain't gonna hurt it none, right?"

"No, that's just insulation. We'll bury the two bags right here, side by side. See? No secrets, Odraye. Remember, we're in this together."

Odraye just fixed him with that same baleful stare. Butchie wondered if he was laying on the palsy-walsy thing a little too heavily. If he dummied it down much more, he'd be talking in Boy Scout code words. Not a safe thing to do with a man like Odraye. His fuse was short enough as it was, and his aggression was compounded by greed.

They killed half a bottle of Jim Beam between them. Odraye lit a blunt and passed it to him. Butchie felt the kick at once, the weed had been soaked in something, maybe formaldehyde or laced with a psychedelic. He hoped it wasn't angel dust. Odraye, he suspected, was testing him, trying to get him loose enough to blab. But Butchie held tight despite the roller-coaster his brain was riding. They gave each other one of those California bro hugs at the door. Lead the bear with honey, not a stick, Yeah, that's the way. . .

Now he had time. Not much but enough to plan it right, think it out this time. The money wasn't going anywhere for now; it would stay put. He had to make sure that wherever he planted Odraye, he'd stay put for a lot longer. Longer as in eternally longer. Butchie liked the ring of that phrase. He heard Nino's echo in his head once again: You can trust him.

Shit, I can only trust him if he's dead, Butchie realized.

CHAPTER 5

"Whadda you want, Butchie?"

Neecie said it all like one word.

"I just wanted to talk to you for a minute. See what's up."

"Nothing. Why? You ain't called me since we broke up—when? Two months ago."

"That long?"

"What's on your mind, Butchie?"

"Can't I just call, you know, say hello?"

"No, not for you. For you, it's gotta be some big deal," Neecie said.

He could hear her sister talking in the background. Lois hated his guts.

"Tell me something."

"What?"

Her heard gum popping; they used to argue about her incessant gum-chewing, a nervous habit he remembered from grade school.

"Did I always used to be—was I always a shit?"

"Hunh?"

"I been thinking about my life lately," Butchie said. He realized how fatuous and stupid that must sound to her. Neecie pulled off scabs. Neecie spat into open wounds.

Neecie laughed; his ancient cell phone added a tinny echo to it.

"Oh, you been thinkin' about your life, have you? It's a little late for that, isn't it?"

Good old Neecie. He'd expected scorn, not sympathy, but still. . .

"Did I ever do things right, I mean. You know, the way they taught us kids."

"Butchie, Butchie. You and you alone are responsible for your life. No one else. Don't blame it on your friends or the streets or this shitty town or anything else. It's you, Butchie. You turned into a selfish sonofabitch. You and you alone wrecked our relationship."

"I wasn't ready to settle down, Neecie."

Christ, that was lame. He could hear the tension gathering in her voice and felt the heat coming through the air; it was like Leotis's spreading halo, mocking him.

"You wasn't ready—Go' damn it, Butchie, you're thirty-three years old. And you're telling me this shit?"

"Neecie, I gotta go. They're paging me over the loudspeaker from the garage."

"Asshole."

"I'll call you again. Maybe we can meet somewhere and talk about it."

"Fuck you. Don't call me again."

What was that old expression of his mother's? Bad always comes to worse. Or worse comes to worse. . . something like that.

The second he heard the robot message from Brockton County Jail, he thought of those sayings.

"It's me," the voice said.

An icy thrill zinged from Butchie's scrotum to his brain: Odraye. Worse: Odraye in jail.

Please God, Butchie silently prayed, please remind him they record all phone calls. . .

"What. . . what are you in for?"

That felt safe enough.

"They picked me up at my place on a bench warrant," Odraye replied. "Some old bullshit."

Some old bullshit could mean anything from Murder One to nonpayment of child support.

"Can you be more specific?" Butchie asked.

The pause seemed like an open gorge across which the seconds were parsed into nanoseconds of time, an eternity of hesitation. Trap, entrapment, his brain screamed. Then Odraye spoke.

"Domestic," Odraye replied. "My girlfriend—my ex-girlfriend decided she's gonna cash in on this Me-Too bullshit."

"Does she—have proof?"

"They told me she showed them some photos. Bitch took selfies and brought 'em in. Fuck, it's her current boyfriend and she's layin' this shit off on me because I threw her skanky ass out for cheatin' on me."

Odraye's voice rose as he got more into it.

The tsunami building in Butchie's stomach subsided to a rogue wave. Thank you, Jesus, he thought. Odraye's performing for the cops; he knows the call is being recorded. This is for show. Nothing to do with that.

"What do you want me to do?" Butchie asked.

"Just callin' to let you know where I'm at," Odraye said noncommittally. "In case, you know."

"Sure," Butchie said. He almost gulped the word. "I'll—I'll see you when you bond out."

"That's the other reason I'm calling, Butchie."

"OK, bail money. I see," Butchie said.

"I know you my friend, like, so I know you can help me out. I'll pay you back, man."

"Sure, that's fine, Odraye. I'll contact a bail bondsman right away. See what I can do."

"Call Petey Martone. He handled me before. He knows I'm good," Odraye said.

No more buddy tone—all business now.

"I'll do that," Butchie said.

"See you, bro."

"See you, bro," Butchie said.

All that bra-bro slang rankled and itched under his skin. Phony, lies. He remembered the nuns' stories in parochial school. They weren't much on science or geography, but goddamn, they could din religion into your ears all day long. Brothers: Cain and Abel; Am I not my brother's keeper? David and Jonathan. Esau and Jacob. Esau, the brutish brother; Jacob grasping his twin's heel as he left the womb. Was James Jesus' brother? He couldn't remember. A vague memory of James tossed off the temple roof flickered across his memory like the seat near the window of that ugly, L-shaped elementary school he sat in. Sun beating through the glass in warm weather, icy winds rattling the panes in winter. He progressed through each room, from grade to grade, like a turd squeezed through the bowels of a monster. At the end, shot out into the streets of Brockton, he was a decent lad in those days before high school. But like the stories of brothers in the Bible the nuns yammered to them, those stories almost always ended in misery and sorrow, rarely happiness.

CHAPTER 6

Butchie's savings account had taken a dump on him thanks to the playoffs and the Superbowl. The days when the Pats engineered their famed comebacks to finish in glory were slipping into fond memories. He used to clear the spread like a deer jumping barbed-wire fence. No more.

Odraye's bail money just about cleaned out what he had left. The thought of using some of that money did occur to him, but it was a thought only, a mere fluttering cabbage moth he blew away at once. That money could not be touched, not until it was safe, no matter what that fool thought.

Butchie knew he didn't have to leave town to get an illegal gun, even as tough as Massachusetts gun laws were. He held a Class B carry license for the Glock 19 he kept in his bedside drawer, but it might as well be a cucumber for all the good it would do if he wanted to carry it on the street and unrelated to the job. The fact Butchie worked some dangerous areas in Brockton allowed him to get the license in the first place, but he couldn't walk around strapped like some aging gangbanger with his ballcap on backwards.

When he talked to his high-school pal Joey De Luca, a trooper who wore his uniform like an SS officer and with as much pride, about whether he ought to apply for a Class A, Joe told him not to bother. They were sitting on bar stools at the Eastside Fratellanza Club, and his former classmate scoffed at the idea.

"Why not?"

"The gun's a tool, Tom. It's just gear. You need the mindset you wanna carry a weapon out here and use it, and you ain't got the mindset, my friend."

He knew Joey was right. He didn't have the mindset. Odraye had the mindset. Whatever enzyme squirted in Butchie's hippocampus that ordered him to fight, flee, or freeze acted differently in him. He remembered falling to the floor in Mrs. Bello's, a victim waiting to have his brains pulped like Leotis Marsten. Even if he had the desire to train for a gun fight, he didn't have the time. What with Odraye coming out of his cage any moment and Asaro, the supervisor, giving him the fisheye at work, he knew something was up. He'd asked Joe to see if he could pick up any scuttlebutt at work.

"Don't know anybody there to call, Butchie. Sorry," Joey said. "I'd help you if I could."

Butchie wondered if a grand jury indictment was coming and he'd be swept up in it. God knows, there was plenty of corruption to go around. Ever since the Godfather films, guys in work clothes and suits walked around the municipal building wondering where they could "wet their beaks" next. Butchie had carved out his niche after ten years on the job—a little kickback here, turn a blind eye there, something to sweeten the report, whatever, it all had worked out until now. Just when he had walked headfirst into the biggest score of his life—of anybody's lifetime—he had managed to handcuff himself to Odraye Suggs, a Neanderthal or a Samson—take your choice—but he could bring down the house either way.

So Butchie did what any felon denied a gun permit did. He flipped a coin: Boston or Providence.

Tails, Providence. Balls McCarthy. . .

He'd have preferred Boston, plenty of his cooms still there resulting from a split in the large Parmenter clan from Naples when they settled there first. Rhode Islanders thought they ruled the country with their New York System Weiners, Del's Lemonade, Mayor "Buddy" Cianci, "No school, Fosta-Glossta" nonsense, whats amatta witchu accent, and coffee milk. He knew a couple bars in providence where somebody could set him up and not ask a dozen questions. Tomorrow night, after Odraye was bonded out and they had another soulful discussion at his place, he'd make a beeline for Interstate 95. Even if Odraye said let's meet at the McDonald's on the corner, he wouldn't go, and he sure as hell wouldn't get into a car with him again unless he had an untraceable weapon on him, conceal-carry license be damned.

"Who drove you here?"

"Somebody I know. Thanks for bailing me out," Odraye said.

He didn't sound grateful.

"Is he gonna wait out there for you?"

Butchie parted the sheers of his picture window and saw the profile of a black male smoking a cigarette, one long bare arm dangled out tapping the side of the car, a white Toyota so mud-daubed it looked as if it had a brown skirt. The rap music inside the car must be deafening if he could hear it from there.

"I ain't got a car," Odraye said. "What am I supposed to do?"

"Uber."

"What?"

"Look, Odraye," Butchie began, weary of pointing out Basic Criminal Practice 101 to his partner, "the fewer the people who know about us, the better."

"Don't worry about it. Let's talk about the money," Odraye demanded.

"I'm taking off work tomorrow. I'm going to see a banker in Quincy tomorrow," Butchie said.

"Quincy? Why go all the way up to Quincy. We got bankers right here," Odraye said.

"It's a reconnaissance," Butchie said. "I want to see what obstacles there are to somebody bringing a quarter-million in outdated cash into a bank."

"What kind of obstacles?"

"Oh, just the usual kind that land us in prison for the next twenty years," Butchie said.

He was tired of playing nurse to a moron. His stomach had a permanent case of butterflies and he was jumping at every strange sound. Yesterday somebody dropped a pipe wrench behind him and he almost jumped out of his skin.

He handed Odraye a beer.

"Banks are where you get cash, or did I miss something?"

"No, you didn't miss anything, but haven't you noticed whenever banks get robbed, the thieves never get away with much cash? It's always like, eight thousand, ten, twelve thousand—never shitloads of money like you see on TV. Banks don't carry much money nowadays. People use credit and debit cards more than cash. Someday there won't be any paper money at all."

"I heard about that Bitcoin bullshit," Odraye said.

"My point is we have to do this right, and we're gonna get, maybe, one chance, see?"

"I'll buy it, Butchie. For now. But I got this feeling you're stalling me. I don't like that feeling, man. When do you get back?"

"I'll call you from Quincy soon as I know anything. We'll know everything by tomorrow afternoon," Butchie said. "When's your next court appearance?"

"Two weeks."

"Plenty of time. Your lawyer any good?"

"Public defender, man. Some white boy just out of law school," Odraye said.

"Can he fuck it up?"

"The courts, man. I been in the system before. Judges and lawyers, they can fuck up a two-car funeral. Why you askin' me?"

"No reason," Butchie said.

Odraye polished off the last of his beer and tossed the empty to Butchie; he headed for the door. Butchie watched the knob disappear inside Odraye's giant fist before Odraye turned around.

"Butchie?"

"Yeah?"

"You ain't stalling me, are you?"

"Stalling you? About what?"

"About the fucking money—what else?"

"No, I'm not. Hey, Odraye. . ."

"Yeah, what?"

"Pack a go-bag just in case."

A few seconds later, Butchie heard a car door slam. The driver cranked up the music. Boorish claims of some rapper throwing shade at an invisible rival about having more "bitches, cars, and cash" boomed out, echoing off the apartment block. The Toyota's sputtering tailpipe popped a staccato counterpoint to the singer's exaggerations as the car passed out of hearing, noisy farts mocking the singer's braggadocio.

CHAPTER 7

Butchie ordered another shot-and-beer combination. The bar was downtown close to Waterplace Park next to another park named for Roger Williams. By then, he'd driven past six places named for Roger Williams. Richie had a hard time remembering who the guy was—something to do with Puritans if the wood-carved, hanging signs in front of shops on South Elmwood were any indication—black loony top hat with a buckle.

The bar, however, was dark and quiet. Only a couple customers at the bar and some couples in the booths. Most looked married except one middle-aged pair whose smiles and constant touching of hands across the table suggested they were on an afternoon tryst.

Half Butchie's mission was accomplished; he'd picked up a small Beretta without much difficulty. He went from one street hustler to another, like a walking tour among the riffraff of downtown Providence, being passed on from a skateboard punk to a street corner derelict to one hustler after another. Finally, some skank with a face scarred from scratching invisible meth bugs, told him Tarvarius could help him out.

"He your boyfriend?" Butchie asked.

"Naw, he's just a guy I know. Come on, man, I'll bring you to him."

They walked down a shabby side street, and she told him to wait at the bottom of the stairs in front of a block of welfare apartments.

Upstairs, through the door, he heard "Bitch, whatchu tell him?" It was followed by her voice, higher-pitched, wheedling. A volley of curses and the door flung open.

Tarvarius in the flesh. He was shirtless, his abdomen six-pack on display, eight inches of white briefs below the belly button.

"Whatchu want with me, bra?"

Butchie was prepared to go through the ritual. The dialogue of "Are you cop/No, I'm not a cop" went on for about twenty minutes before he disappeared back up the stairs inside the apartment. Five minutes passed before he emerged again, taking the stairs with the agility of a mountain goat. He led Butchie under the stairwell. From a blanket tucked under his arm, Tarvarius unfolded his wares like an Arab in a souk: three pieces, all with the numbers filed off, as if cops didn't know forensics and wouldn't apply acid to lift the numbers back into view.

Butchie bypassed the Sig and a handsome, new-looking silver-and-black Taurus with a snubbed hammer for the Pico .380. Light and concealable, the gun would go in an ankle holster or behind his belt. He handed him a wad of twenties and fifties, three hundred, the asking price.

He'd taken a half-dozen steps before he felt a tug on his triceps.

"Hey, motherfucker, you said you'd give me a finder's fee!"

"Sorry," Butchie replied. "Here you go."

He handed her two twenties, folded into a tight triangle like a prison "kite" convicts used for exchanging messages on strings.

Dopers, Butchie thought, they'd knock their own grandmothers to the sidewalk if she was standing on a dollar bill. Then an image of Mrs. Bello, a woman dead while he was making his Confirmation, rose to mind. Somehow his brain filled in the image for a woman he'd never seen—babushka-type, stocky build like a Boston stevedore, gibbering in a mushy-voweled mix of Italian and English.

God, I'm one to talk about knocking over grandmas. . .

But the conversation at the bank had not gone well and he needed time to think before he called Odraye about it. The bank manager he'd called had the impression Butchie was talking about mutilated currency and suggested he fill out a standard form. Butchie told him it was a different kind of problem, he said.

"It's money from a relative," Butchie said.

He'd rehearsed the story on the drive up: poor old demented Aunt Clara. She lived alone, was a hoarder, too, unfortunately, and when she died recently, the family—my two cousins, that is, ha-ha—called me and asked me if I knew of a bank in Quincy, which is where they're from originally, you know, and—and fuck, shit, piss—nobody would buy this stupid crock of shit for a minute. . . His only hope was if the manager's corrupt, willing to take a percentage. He'd deal with Odraye's objections later.

The manager of the First Third of Quincy gave him the fisheye.

"Are these notes outdated? Is that what you're saying, Mister—"

"Reese," Butchie said. "John Reese."

"Do you have the dates on the banknotes?"

"Ha-ha, no, sorry. I'm just running an errand for my cousins. They know I travel through Quincy on my route every week. See, I'm a long-hauler. I carry mostly iron coil."

Bullshit, bullshit. . .

It was the one bank in Quincy not hooked into a national bank where the contact would have to be reported, or so Butchie guessed. That was why he avoided Boston banks; they existed in the FBI's backyard. No sense stirring up that pot of shit unless he had no other choice.

Butchie did, in fact, do some online checking and discovered collectors valued the silver-backed dollar notes, but he didn't know if there were that many in the garbage bags, and he didn't want to get into third-party transactions—too risky. He was surprised to learn there were exchangers and dealers who would buy the money to make more on the exchange with a bank. He found several websites advertising their services; they'd buy money in bulk and exchange it with major banks, but their rates were as exorbitant as the vigorish on the street. Butchie wasn't sure how much or what percentage of the total they possessed was defunct. He kept this as an option in reserve and hoped, if it came to that, he could find somebody crooked enough to take on the job but not too greedy to demand a huge cut.

He never told Odraye that this branch in Quincy was the only one he'd found within a couple hundred miles of Brockton that acknowledged exchanging phased-out currency on its website. When he broached the subject of the bank taking a small percentage—Butchie mentioned 5%, "for your time, of course, sir," the manager shot him a look much closer to the infamous malocchio. The guy's name was Kevin O'Something. Butchie and his friends had a long history with the neighborhood Micks. "Italians and Irish," his father said, "they get along like cats and dogs in a burlap sack."

Leaving the bank, he mused over the irony of it; here he was trying to bring a couple hundred thousand dollars into a bank, not take out that amount like a robber, and it was becoming a dull headache. Not to mention having an anxious partner waiting for news back in Brockton. Odraye was acting crazier than a two-headed dog in a meat market. Bank robbers weren't the only ones being disadvantaged by the modern-day addiction to plastic money.

A new bartender swung by to check his drink. He hadn't noticed that the thirty-something male with the blue glyph on his neck had been replaced by a pretty young woman whose tee exposed a huge amount of midriff flesh. The lettering on her chest was distorted by the distension her breasts produced; he could make out what it said without all the letters: Don't Bother I'm Not Drunk Yet.

"Refill, Mister?"

"Ouch, that makes me feel so old."

She laughed, exposing even white teeth. Her pink lipstick was almost fluorescent. Blonde, butter-colored hair in that shaggy style that made girls look as if they'd just stepped out of the shower.

"Go ahead," Butchie said, "a double this time, no chaser. Have one on me."

Six more doubles later, Butchie was leaning over the fender of his Wrangler tossing up most of the whisky. His head throbbed, and it was beginning to rain. He was almost dead broke now. His last twenty went for a tip to the pretty barmaid, a twenty-two-year-old named something that sounded like "Seychelles," but had to be something else. As more customers came in, especially the younger guys with their high-and-tight buzzcuts or ponytails, she found Butchie less and less interesting no matter how much he tipped over the cost of the drinks he bought. Played by a girl, a child, for God's sake. Neecie was right to complain about him. The old Irish priests Brockton had to import from Ireland to replace the priests who died, retired, or got kicked out for being pederasts were right about something else, too: young men were led around by their cocks, not their brains, and the devil never stopped working through that particular part of the male anatomy.

He got inside the Jeep while the rain increased its tempo against the windshield, a perfect ending to a shitty day.

"You drunk, motherfucker?"

"I've had a few," Butchie admitted.

When he tried to summarize what the branch manager of the bank had told him, he bollixed it up and slurred too many words.

"You kill yourself on the road home tonight," Odraye said. "I'll make sure you get a nice funeral with your share."

Money was never far from Odraye's linguistic radar.

"Thash—that's mighty kind of you, Odraye."

"Fuck you, Butchie. We gonna be talking come the morning, first fuckin' thing, and you better be sober, motherfucker."

He ended the connection.

"Well, that went well," Butchie said to nobody but the damp night air of Quincy in his Jeep. He pushed the dome light with his palm and blinked several times, as if that would generate sobriety. He tossed the phone onto the passenger seat. He adjusted the mirror to take in his face and noted the bloodshot eyes, the heavy shadow of his beard, the tousled hair, thinning too fast like his old man's.

Butchie wasn't superstitious. He hadn't darkened the threshold of a church since he and Neecie split up. She was a believer and constantly reminded him "He was watching" whenever Butchie's footsteps were inclined to wander from the straight-and-narrow. But just then, rubbing his grizzled jaw while he stared at his reflection, he hoped his queasy stomach wouldn't revolt again and he didn't weave in his lane on the drive back so that some trooper like Joe De Luca pulled him over. If that happened, he'd blurt out the whole sordid catastrophe of the last week—Leotis, the sledgehammer, the money—all of it, and let them drag him off like a dog to prison where they could bury him inside a steel cage in Walpole until it was time for the back-door parole or the stainless-steel ride.

Lethal injection or death from old age in a prison—hideous alternatives, a hell on earth just to contemplate. They were also a fast way for Butchie to buck himself up, exhale a few deep breaths, slam the Jeep into drive, and exit the parking lot for the highway.

Some things you're ready for, and some things you're not, he told the mirror.

CHAPTER 8

Butchie offered the man a drink. If he'd had his wits about him, he realized too late, he'd have asked for the guy's business card and told him he'd call him later. As it was, he let him inside and it was too late to do anything about it.

The guy was big, even taller than Odraye but not as stocky. A gym rat from the looks of the deltoids straining his polo shirt. The tiny green alligator on his chest looked happy, like a kid's idea of an alligator, not one of those 15-foot dragons that yanked a five-hundred-pound zebra trying to ford the Zambezi River.

"Do you have a card on you?" Butchie asked, thinking he might recover some ground after being such a pushover and letting the guy in while he was still half-asleep. The booze fog hadn't yet lifted; he knew his breath must smell like the sewer pipe in the animal rendering plant where his grandfather worked just off the boat.

"No," the man said, "but I have this."

He had the private investigator badge already palmed, and he flipped it toward Butchie. Even if Butchie's eyes weren't clouded with too much drink and too little sleep, he couldn't have read it from that distance.

"Name's Hoyt, Dominic Hoyt."

"That's what this card says," Butchie replied looking up.

Hoyt shrugged. "This is America. You are who you say you are."

"And who are you?"

"I'm a private investigator hired by the Bello family. I'm looking into the possible disappearance of money from the estate of Mrs. Orazia Bello, the grandmother."

"I see. Can you wait here a second? I've got to throw some water on my face."

"Late night?"

"I had to work late," Butchie said.

He heard Hoyt call from the foyer: "I understand you're the housing inspector for Mrs. Bello's section."

Prick, can't wait a second for me to clear my head. Butchie stared at his face in the bathroom mirror. He looked a mess, all right, worse than he thought. He had ragged dreams all night until dawn. Then this big jerk comes pounding on the door. . .

"Sorry about that," Butchie said, returning, forcing a smile. "I was racking up some good Z's when you knocked."

"My apologies, Mister Parmenter. I won't take up much of your time."

"Sure, what can I do for you?"

"Mrs. Bello's store was recently condemned by you as housing inspector, am I correct?"

"Yes, I made that decision. It's in my report. We'd had complaints from the neighbors. Bricks falling in, junkies crashing in the place, broken windows. It was way past eyesore," Butchie replied.

"I understand. The family didn't want to tear down the property until they'd made a thorough search for the money. I take it you're aware of the fact Mrs. Bello never used banks and kept all the money she'd accumulated over fifty years somewhere inside the store?"

Decision time.

"No, I didn't know that. I don't live that close to the neighborhood, and I don't know any of the Bello family personally."

"I see," Hoyt replied. "But you're not surprised?"

"Lots of people didn't trust banks in those days, so no, I'm not surprised. My own grandmother didn't trust banks."

Careful, careful, Butchie. Don't go overboard with the helpful citizen act here. . .

Hoyt's head was huge and ringed with dozens of tiny curls that lay flat against his head as if he'd just come from a ladies' salon. It reminded Butchie of cherubs on Christmas cards, those fat little baby angels with wings. He held a small notebook in his hand and flicked pages, licking his index finger to turn pages. Neecie had that disgusting habit until he begged her to stop. Hoyt kept flicking pages, casually reading, not in any big hurry.

"Is there something I can help you with?"

Patience, Butchie, don't show him anything—

Hoyt suddenly looked up. Butchie couldn't read the grin on his face.

"Do you know of anyone named Leotis Marsten?"

"No, sorry."

"He's missing. His mother lives across the street from the old Bello place. She runs a hair-styling shop. Does hair for the women in the neighborhood. She's reported him gone all of a sudden."

"And?"

"And Leotis, according to my sources here"—Hoyt tapped the notebook—"all say Leotis never strayed far from home. Lived with his mother. Ran errands for her. Practically a recluse. They also say he never went anywhere on his own, these people I talked to. No job. Collected SSI. Always told his mother everything he did."

"Sounds like a Momma's boy," Butchie replied.

"Yes, it does."

Hoyt's grin revealed small teeth, an unsettling contrast to his size.

"So you think this Leotis found the money and took off?"

Hoyt made a wry face, thinking it over, like a gambler at a blackjack table assessing the odds of a third card.

"No. No, frankly I don't. He wasn't that kind of person. I'm good at reading people, Thomas."

"Butchie."

"I'm sorry?"

"My name. Nobody calls me Thomas."

"I see. Well, I have a theory I'm working on. I think Leotis Marsten might know something about that hidden money, but he might be in a situation where he can't talk about it to anyone."

"You think he was kidnapped—is that what you mean?"

The guy must have been a cop in another life, Butchie thought. They toss you a crumb and expect you to bleed out your life story.

"Possibly. But maybe not. We'll have to see if he's a loose end or not, maybe collateral damage or just an innocent explanation for why a man who's tied to his mother's apron strings for thirty-five years suddenly decides to take off without a word to her or anyone in the neighborhood."

"OK, well, good luck in your investigation, Mister Hoyt, but if you'll excuse me, I've got to get ready for work now."

"Of course, Butchie. I want to thank you for your cooperation in the matter. If you like, I can let you know how things turn out."

"That's OK," Butchie replied.

Hoyt suddenly lunged toward him.

Butchie held his ground and didn't flinch. Either his senses were too dulled from the hangover or he'd already had some practice with big men threatening moves, all thanks to Odraye Suggs.

Hoyt stopped just short of invading Butchie's space and held out his hand.

"I appreciate the time," Hoyt said and shot him that grin again, more like a sneer.

Butchie shook his hand. His own was dry. Another gift from the dehydration of last night's bender.

Hoyt opened the glass door and suddenly stopped; he made a half-turn without looking directly at Butchie.

"I'm surprised," Hoyt said, turning in the doorway.

"Surprised?"

"Yeah. You didn't ask me how much the old lady had hidden away."

"How much?"

Hoyt gave him that same sly grin and walked down the steps. A big man in no hurry.

Son of a bitch, Butchie cursed. Now I got to go deal with Odraye.

Butchie's immediate problem how to break the news was solved by his supervisor's message on his answering service; he stated if Butchie didn't show up again without a doctor's excuse, he was being docked three days' pay "per civil servant contract rules."

Odraye listened while Butchie told him about Quincy, although he left out the parts about getting a gun and then getting drunk. Odraye took it better than he expected. Being in a public place would help keep a lid on Odraye's temper for a while, Butchie hoped.

He didn't curse much when Butchie told him they'd have to look for another bank and "might have to give up a very small percentage" to get it done with no paperwork or electronic trail back to them.

"I don't give a fuck about no trail," Odraye said. "I'm bustin' outta this shithole town."

Not soon enough, Butchie thought.

Butchie had picked a neutral site to meet, but the BAT station garage on Center was beginning to thin out. Still, hiding in plain sight seemed best. He was on lunch break and had several housing apartments nearby.

"We got us another problem," Butchie said.

"God damn, Butchie, all I ever hear you say is 'We got us another problem.' When you gonna start solvin' problems, motherfucker?"

Odraye, the pressure-cooker time bomb. Butchie didn't think his partner in crime could keep a cork in it much longer. Odraye was right: they had to start solving problems and soon.

Butchie told him about Hoyt's visit that morning.

"Fuck that motherfucker!"

"I don't think that family gathering over there by the pillar heard you. Want to say it a little louder?"

It was like some fairy tale in reverse: he was shedding twenty-dollar bills like tissue off a roll of toilet paper while a fortune sat uselessly stored up in his garage loft. He could try to spend it but there was a real chance his partner would bring down the house once he had his mitts on that much cash. It galled Butchie to call that psycho Odraye his "partner"; it was like calling Jeffrey Dahmer a chef. He was that loose cannon on deck everybody talked about. People were coming at Butchie from all directions because Odraye killed the harmless Leotis Marsten instead of piecing him off with a share of the money. He had just as much right to it as Butchie himself or Odraye—only a pathetic thief's right. Butchie felt like a newly hatched gecko with a bunch of racer snakes coming after him. He had no clue where to turn next.

"Where are you staying now?" Butchie asked him.

"My boy Diz puttin' me up 'til I get squared away," Odraye replied.

"He's the one who dropped you off yesterday?"

"Yeah, so what? What's with the twenty questions, man? They got me locked out of my apartment. Taped a notice from the court on the door. Didn't even wait for me to make bail. I can't get in."

Butchie breathed a sigh of relief. A quit notice from the court wasn't significant.

"Best not go near your old place for a while, I'm thinking," Butchie said. "Can you promise me you'll do that much while I work on a plan?"

"Stop fuckin' the dog, Butchie. Get this thing solved or I will."

He remained sitting on the bench, his hands folded in front of him, like a dozen of others milling about, waiting for bus service. Over his shoulder, Butchie watched a man step out of the shadows behind a post and join Odraye, a smaller man with a cocky swagger, lean brown limbs and a lit cigarette cupped in one hand in defiance of all the No Smoking signs in the place. He adjusted his gait to Odraye's, a shadow hidden by the bigger man's profile.

Another snake added to the mix.

Butchie turned in his report forms and stopped by his supervisor's desk. An embossed name plate said Daniel P. Asaro. The P was for Pasqualone. Too cheap to put all the letters in.

"You wanted to see me?"

"Have a seat, Parmenter."

"Thanks, I'll stand."

"We had a call yesterday while you were off on a personal day."

"Off sick," Butchie corrected.

"We had a call from a woman." A long pause and then he said the name: "Delores Negrón."

Asaro waited, looking at him.

He wants me to burst into some hysterical explanation defending myself, Butchie thought. Or else he's secretly taping me.

"I know who she is," Butchie said. "What of it?"

"She claims you assaulted her when you were inspecting the Jones property on Wayman Avenue. That was Tuesday, last week. What do you have to say to it?"

"I say she's lying," Butchie said. "She's trying to shake me down. I want to talk to a lawyer before I say anything to you."

Fluorescent light gleamed off the top of Asaro's head.

"You made a big mistake this time, Parmenter. But, then, since I've known you, I suspect you've broken a few other regulations, haven't you?"

"Have I? What regulations?" Butchie decided to give him nothing, but he thought: Here we go straight into a clusterfuck. . .

"Soliciting sex from anyone on the job—that's a fireable offense, quite likely you're facing a criminal prosecution to boot."

Asaro looked smug. He made a tent of his fingers and smiled at Butchie. "You're suspended as of today. A hearing is scheduled for next week. You'll need to turn in any equipment you've signed out and your pro rata seniority is also being tolled."

Butchie didn't understand the last part and didn't care.

"What do I do?"

"Go home," Asaro said. "I suspect the police will want to talk to you soon."

Asaro used to be a notorious womanizer on the job. Every female dispatcher was warned about him and he was written up once, if scuttlebutt was true. He'd taken a month off recently to undergo chemotherapy for testicular cancer. Word around the building was he'd found religion.

Still, there he was, Butchie thought, a pot calling the kettle black.

He felt trapped in his father's sayings. But there were bigger traps out there, and he would have to negotiate the twisting maze they lay hidden in with a blindfold on. And he was running out of time.

CHAPTER 9

Butchie pulled up in front of her apartment complex. Terracotta belied the basic simplicity of design: three cement-block rectangles piled on top of each other, Soviet style. The frou-frou latticework out front gave curbside appeal and nothing else.

He climbed the same steps as he had on last Tuesday's inspection. Back then, he had no worries. She had come on to him right away, flirting like a schoolgirl, wrapping the loose belt of her white terrycloth robe around her whenever it slipped down her hips. She followed him from room to room, smiling as he went, clipboard in hand, once peering at him from the bedroom doorway, one hand on her cocked hip.

Then she slowly let her fingers undo the belt and gave Butchie a good look at her sex, the nub of clitoris appearing between the cleft and upward to the trimmed Mohawk of her pubic ruff. Like a camera eye, Butchie's gaze traveled upward as the robe came all the way off and she stood there with her breasts exposed, ruby nipples distended like erasers.

In seconds, she was helping him remove his belt and then she was holding him by the hips as she sunk to her knees and took him in her mouth. Butchie had not had sex in months—so much for the single bachelor in Brockton. He'd given up on the bar scene and stayed home to drink. This, now, was bliss and he let her guide him to her bed. The romp was over in minutes. Butchie's celibacy exploded in a gush.

He remembered they kissed at the doorway. He wrote her cell number down, said he'd call her soon, and that was that. Casual sex at its best—no frills, no worries. She gave as good as she got, and Butchie assumed he was probably one in a long line of lucky males who benefited from a house call that way. No big deal. The only thing that nagged at him was the fact she never asked whether he had a condom or suggested he use one. But, then, that was her call, not his.

Now this.

He gave three quick raps on her door, Number 106.

The door opened on a chain lock; the catch slid on the track to allow him to see half her face.

"What do you want?"

"Delores, it's me, Butchie."

"You shouldna be here," she said.

"We need to talk," he said. "Will you let me in?"

She slammed the door shut.

He rapped on the door again. She shouted though it: "Go away before I call the cops!"

Butchie retreated. Two small, light-skinned Puerto Ricans, a boy and girl with identical mocha eyes and thick mops of curly black hair, watched him from the bottom of the steps. He felt their eyes boring into his back as he headed to his Jeep.

He'd walked up and down stairs like this in housing units like this past children at play a hundred times. Now he felt like somebody trying to make a house of cards under strobe lighting.

The dirty white Toyota picked him up at the intersection of North Montebello. He kept glancing in the mirror to see if Odraye was sitting in the passenger seat, but it appeared to be just Diz, the smoker.

Odraye keeping tabs on him, worried about the money. . .

"Go ahead and follow me, you mutt," Butchie said into the mirror. With all his mounting worries, having a tail didn't amount to much of a concern.

He parked in his reserved spot and fetched his mail and the daily paper from his mailbox in the alcove adjacent to his section of the complex. He walked up the steps. The business card tucked into the glass frame said: Det. Raymond E.

Forshey, below that: Major Crimes, followed by the precinct address on Commercial Street.

In ballpoint pen, the time, 4:10 p.m. was noted and lastly, two words: Call me.

Butchie poured himself a drink and stripped off his shirt and undid his belt; he paced in his living room and flicked the card with his fingernail as he paced, thinking of the pros and cons of not calling right away.

The big pro to not calling was his nerve-shot state of mind after losing his job and Delores' bizarre behavior. He might blurt something out. The con was that the longer he delayed, the more likely he was hiding something could be the detective's assumption. Innocent people don't lawyer up and they don't hide from the police.

Butchie threw back a long slug of the whiskey and let it scorch its way down his throat. It hit his belly and sent vectors of heat in all directions outward from the trunk until it reached his fingertips and the hair on his scalp. He thought of following that with another but changed his mind. He dialed the number instead.

"Detectives. Officer Robinson speaking."

"I have a card. I mean, Detective Forshey left his card at my place. He asked me to call this number."

"OK, what is your name, sir?"

"Parmenter. My name's Parmenter."

"I'll have him call you as soon as he comes in."

Mind games, Butchie thought.

The newspaper had come unfolded on the coffee table. The article about Leotis Marsten's body found in the abandoned building was above the fold on page 3. Butchie's eyes zig-zagged through the two-column article, trying to glean any pertinent details when the phone rang.

"Detective Forshey, Mister Parmenter."

"Yes, hello, Detective."

"Will you be home tonight? I'd like to drop by to discuss a case I'm working on."

Butchie squeezed his eyes shut and grimaced into the

phone but kept his voice even: "Sure, I'll be here."

"See you about eight?"

"That'll be fine."

Fuck a duck.

CHAPTER 10

Odraye's cell rang but it went to voicemail again. Butchie left no message. From being a constant nag and threat, Odraye had suddenly become as reclusive as a badger. Butchie doubted his formidable partner was a regular subscriber to The Enterprise. He had to trust to word on the street to communicate this latest development through its own system of jungle drums, which generally meant the gossip of males in bars.

During his longest drinking bout, Butchie became friendly with Bobby Steele, the only person he knew who seemed to live out the destiny of his name; three tours in Iraq, two more in Afghanistan, Bobby had accumulated enough metal in his corpus from a roadside explosion outside Kunar to set off a bat's sonar detector, never mind the airport metal detectors. He had a prosthetic leg, a missing hand, and still considered himself the best mixologist in Brockton.

Bittaker's had gone through several transformations over the decades from a creepy lounge-lizard establishment with a red-black décor and frilly drapes through a decade as a yuppie fern bar to its current status as a biker bar; it looked as though it had finally found its proper place in life like water seeking its equilibrium. The name had changed, too, from Mango's to The Bulldogger (an unintended signal to lesbians who referred to their prison relationships that way) and finally, to Bittaker's Bar. Locals first called it "Two-Bits Bittaker's" because of a game involving some late-night shenanigans with some of the rougher clientele making bets to see who bought drinks. The one with the fewest quarters bought. That ended when the rules required the opposing guy's girlfriend to remove the quarters and fights started breaking out.

"Hey, Bobby."

"Butchie, long time and all that shit. Whiskey and a water back, am I right?"

"You got it."

Butchie didn't want to drink but ordering a club soda wasn't going to ingratiate himself and he didn't want to appear needy. He and Bobby talked Red Sox and Bruins for a few minutes.

"What brings you back, Butchie? I heard you were on the wagon," Bobby said.

"Yeah, I tried sobriety for a while, but my life was just as fucked up."

"You complainin'?"

"Naw. Just saying."

Bobby flexed the fingers of his artificial hand. Butchie was one of many customers gulled into a bet that Bobby could pick up an egg and crush a beer can with it.

"You should see the latest model of this," Bobby said. "Advanced military design. This shit's right up there with Luke Skywalker's bionic hand—you know, after his old man whacks it off with the crimson sword."

"I must have missed that one."

Bobby had what the World Health Organization called "gaming disorder"; his Call of Duty episodes were binges that lasted for three days straight with only piss breaks and time out for munchies.

"Bobby, you heard about the body found in that shithole building?"

"Some guys were in here talking about it. It was in the papers."

"You know anything about the victim?"

"Why you asking me?"

"Just curious," Butchie replied. "It was me that condemned the place a few weeks back. I'm wondering how I missed it."

"Must have happened after you were in there. Black dude,

some neighborhood guy. He wasn't a fiend, so the cops think it was connected to the money."

"You mean that story of the old lady hiding a fortune in the walls—some shit like that?"

"No story, man. The cops are convinced the money was there and somebody made off with it. The family hired a dude from Boston to look into it."

"Some gumshoe?"

"Nope. Guy's a merc from what I hear at the bar, guys talkin'. Ex-military, they say, Special Ops. Those are badasses you do not want to fuck with."

Serious props from a combat engineer like Bobby, Butchie thought. Not good, not good at all.

"Where are you?"

"I'm in a bar on Montebello," Butchie said. "Bittaker's. You know it? I've been trying to call you."

"What about?"

"Oh, just to catch up, you know, talk about the weather, say what up," Butchie said.

"You a real smartass, you know that? You want to go a few rounds with me sometime, Mister Smart Ass? I can teach you to stop jerking me around."

"Look, we have—"

"Don't you fuckin' start that 'We have a problem' shit or I'll come down to that redneck bar and bust your ass up."

"We have a situation," Butchie resumed. "I'm supposed to be home in an hour to meet with the detective who's investigating a certain deed involving certain parties—"

"Cut the shit, motherfucker, and say it," Odraye fumed.

"We need to be sure we're in sync every step of the way from here on."

Butchie thought of Bobby's wiggling fingers opening in front of him like a tarantula's legs. "We got to be like the fingers of one hand, as Booker T. used to say." Or was it the peanut guy, George Washington Carver. Maybe MLK said that. . .

"What the fuck are you talking about?"

"It's a metaphor," Butchie said. The nuns at least would be proud of him.

"You—you tryin' my patience, Butchie! You never talked to cops before? You don't fuckin' tell them anything. That's how you do it."

"It's a murder investigation, Odraye, not jaywalking. It's called LWOP. You heard of that, right, with all your vast criminal and cop experiences? Life without parole, and I am not going into the jug because you think you can outsmart da po-lice."

Oops. Maybe a bridge too far there—

Odraye ignored the slur. "Calm your ass down. Go home and sober up."

"I'm not drunk. I'm worried about what they know," Butchie said.

"They don't know shit because you ain't gonna tell 'em shit, are you? Or are you that stupid? They start reading Miranda at you, you say, 'No thanks, Officer, sir, I prefer not to talk' and you stand up and walk out of there. Man up, motherfucker! What's wrong with you? Call me when the cop leaves and don't use your fuckin' cell phone."

It was the longest conversation he'd had with Odraye since the murder. Butchie was shocked to realize it, but his advice was sound. Once they used their wiles to get him in that tiny interrogation room, they'd apply all that cop psychology to pick him apart. One of the lawyers who worked in the legal affairs division called the weakness in a case the "pink underbelly." Between him and Odraye, he was the pink underbelly, not the actual murderer. It didn't matter. He was just as guilty of the murder now, and it didn't matter if he'd been sitting outside in the city vehicle while it happened. His chance for redemption came and went the moment he took the sledgehammer from Suggs. Time to man up, as Odraye said.

He got off the stool when he felt a hand grip his shoulder.

"Hey, Anthony, what's up?"

Shit, Neecie's brother. Both siblings despised Butchie.

The two guys flanking Anthony DiGiacomo were Devil's Disciples from their patch: a skeleton riding a chopper and on the skeleton's helmet a tiny red swastika.

"I want to have a word with you."

"Sure, Anthony."

"Not here, you guys," Bobby said.

"We'll step outside, Bobby," Anthony said. "No problem, hey. C'mon, Butchie."

Butchie looked at Bobby and said, "It's OK. We're friends."

Outside the traffic on Montebello was thinning out after rush hour.

"I know you think—"

Butchie never finished the sentence. The two bikers had him in a high-low takedown, convict style. When he was pulled to his feet, Butchie felt an arm bar around his neck and his arms pinned by the other biker.

"Stay the fuck away from Denise, ricchione motherfucker!"

Butchie couldn't reply if he wanted to.

"Let him go," Anthony said.

The chokehold eased up; he could breathe again. The biker in front of him patted him on the chest. "You're cool, right?"

"Cool," Butchie choked out.

Some signal was exchanged among the three men, and Anthony replaced the biker facing him. Butchie just had time to notice Anthony's right hand was silver when it described a short arc and snapped upwards clipping him under the jaw.

The punch would have knocked him to the sidewalk again except that the biker behind him propped him up and held him.

"You all right? You all right?"

A voice, not Anthony's.

"Yeah . . . I'm. . . fine."

"That's good. You do what the brother says now, you hear?"

When his vision cleared, he saw Anthony's contorted face.

The glob of spit hit him in the forehead, a thick hawker. It was the first time he'd ever been spat upon.

Still woozy, Butchie watched the three men walk north on Montebello. When he felt his legs steady enough, he went back inside.

Bobby was serving a customer at one end of the bar. He saw Butchie and came over.

"What was that all about?"

"Just family stuff," Butchie said.

"Another shot-and-beer?"

"Nope, better not. Got to see a man about a horse," Butchie said. Another dumbass saying of his father's. He opened his wallet and took out one of his last three twenties and laid it on the bar top.

"Thanks, Bobby."

"You OK, Butchie? You look like you seen a ghost."

"I'm looking at him now," Butchie said.

He stared at himself in the cracked bar mirror.

Det. Forshey was anything but intimidating in size. He was barely five-seven. He had an old-time movie-star moustache like Errol Flynn. Butchie remembered his dad had loved some old black-and-white pirate movie the actor starred in.

"How did he die?" Butchie asked. "Or is that information you're holding back from the public?"

"On no, it's too late for that," Forshey replied. "His head was bashed in. A heavy, blunt instrument, the M.E. says. Most likely a sledge or a thick pipe. His brains leaked through his nostrils. It was a pretty good swing. Whoever did it really put his hips into it."

Butchie assumed that was cop humor.

"What happened to your face?"

"I slipped on the steps coming home late last night," Butchie said.

"Looks fresh—I mean, the wound. It looks recent."

"It was in the wee hours, very late, close to dawn."

Butchie mimed drinking.

"You often drink to excess, Mister Parmenter?"

Said with a smile but there was intent behind the question.

"I'd just broken up with my girlfriend."

Butchie shrugged his shoulders: What else is a guy to do but get shit-faced?

"It must have hurt pretty bad," Forshey said. He licked his pencil tip and wrote in his notebook.

What is it with people, Butchie wondered. Their damn notebooks, like dogs constantly licking.

"The fall?"

"No," Forshey replied. "I meant the break-up. Lots of homicides happen right after a girl breaks up with a guy."

"I'm sure."

"You were there, I understand."

"Yes, I condemned the place."

"What date was that?"

"Uh, it's in my report," Butchie said. "Tuesday, week before last."

"That was the last time you were there?"

"Yes," Butchie said.

Too late. Maybe Anthony's punch had given him a slight concussion.

"No, wait, let me correct that. I was there this past Friday. It was my last call, I think. I was giving the place a final walk-through."

"This was after you had already condemned it?"

"Yes."

Of course, he'd been seen in the street that day. All three of them, no doubt. What was he thinking?

"Is it standard practice to condemn a building then go back to it? Why would you do that?"

"It's—it's not standard practice in every instance," Butchie said. "I will return sometimes in case there's an immediate fire or pedestrian hazard or if the building has equipment inside that needs to be removed or any hazardous waste before it can be demolished."

"Does the owner of the building have to pay for the work?"

"Well, that's a legal question," Butchie said. "You're taking me out of my depth. Sometimes the lawyers get involved and sometimes the city confiscates—I mean, appropriates—property to recoup expenses."

"Was that what it was in this case? Lawyers appropriating it for the city? Or is the family paying for it?"

"You'd have to ask my supervisor, Pat Asaro. He'd know. I just do what I'm told."

"Just a foot soldier, huh? I spoke to Mister Asaro. He says you're in some difficulty with lawyers yourself. Is that right?"

"It's personal. I'd prefer not to talk about it."

. . . No thanks, Officer, sir, I prefer not to talk to you about jackshit. . .

"I see."

Butchie watched the detective scribble in his notebook. He gripped the armrest of the davenport to keep his hand from twitching.

"So what were you and Leotis Marsten talking about in front of the Bello place on Friday?"

"Well, I knew you were going to ask and I didn't want to. . . . to admit to it. You see, Leotis came over and asked if he could take the refrigerator inside the building. He wanted it for his mother, he said. He offered me ten bucks and I said he could take it. It was theft of city property and I didn't want to get into trouble if it got out."

"I see. I thought maybe you didn't want to tarnish the memory of the deceased," Forshey said.

"That too."

"Who was the other man with you? Does he work for the city too?"

"I don't know him. A big guy. He was with Leotis. He was there to lift the fridge. Hey, I sold it. I know I shouldn't have but I wasn't about to carry the damn thing for him."

"Witnesses said the big man, an African-American male, between two-fifty and two-ninety, well over six feet. They said he was with you, not Leotis Marsten. They were sure of that."

"Nope, not true," Butchie said. "Never saw him before that

day. He came with Leotis. Leotis introduced himself but not that guy. Just said he was there to help lift the fridge. I said 'Fine,' and that was it."

"Why didn't he take the refrigerator then? It's still there," Forshey said.

This time, he stopped writing in his notebook and stared at Butchie, a cop's auger stare, not a questioning look.

"Hell, I don't know," Butchie replied. "I pocketed the money and asked them to shut the door behind them on their way out. I didn't want to be a part of it so I left when I made my walk-through."

Please, please, please God, don't let any witnesses say they saw Odraye in my truck. . .

"That refrigerator," Forshey said, "it was moved. You can see the scrape marks on the floorboards and where the dust was disturbed. It was moved and then it was shoved back."

"Maybe Leotis and the big man he was with, they must have done it. I don't know."

"Three sets of prints," Forshey said. "It looks like somebody tried to scuff up the prints but they're there, all right. Plain as can be. I have the photos."

"I can't help you there, Detective," Butchie said. "I was long gone by then. Some of those prints would be mine, of course. That's my job."

"Of course."

"Anything else I can help you with, Officer?"

Wrong, wrong—don't say that—

"Just a couple more questions, Mister Parmenter. Did you go upstairs?"

"Yes."

"On both days? The Tuesday, the day you inspected the building and this past Friday when you—re-inspected the building?"

"Yes, I believe so. Yes, that's right, I did."

"On your second visit did you notice anything different?"

"How. . . different?"

"Things out of place, signs of people having been inside,

maybe some damage that wasn't there that Tuesday?"

"No, it looked the same. Junkies, crackheads, taggers—you know. There could have been any number of people inside between that Tuesday and Friday. I wouldn't know. I wasn't looking for that kind of thing, how many more food wrappers lying around, you know. The place is a dump. It should have been torn down ten, fifteen years ago."

"What did you do with the money you found behind the refrigerator?"

"W-what?"

"Just pulling your leg, Mister Parmenter. You know about the hidden money old lady Bello stashed away. It's practically a Brockton legend."

"No, I mean, yeah, sure, I'm—I was aware of it. I think Leotis even talked about it, mentioned it in passing. Made a joke about finding it in there—inside the fridge."

Detective Forshey's eyes drilled Butchie. "Seems to me, if I thought there was even a particle of a chance that a couple hundred thousand dollars was squirreled away inside that refrigerator, I'd have stripped it down to scrap metal right there and then. Every nut and bolt. But you gave it away for ten dollars just like that," Forshey said and snapped his fingers.

"Well, it was just a story," Butchie said. "I didn't put any stock in it. I'm sure Mrs. Bello, if she had that kind of money, she'd have found a much better hiding spot for it."

"You never know, do you? Well, I thank you for your time, Mister Parmenter. You have my card if you think of anything else?"

"Anything else?"

"Somebody suspicious in the neighborhood, somebody hanging around the store who doesn't belong there. Somebody lurking around the building at an odd time, that kind of thing."

He means a white man like me. He means me.

"How'd it go? God damn it, boy, you took your good old

fuckin' time."

"If they ever bring back the Walmart greeter, you should apply," Butchie said.

"What did the cop say?"

"He had questions. I answered them. Normal questions. People know I was there. I'm on record as being there. I had to tell him why I came back to the Bello store if I'd already condemned it."

"What he say?"

"It's fine, no problem," Butchie said. "I covered it, like I said, but I had to say I spoke to you and Leotis—"

"You did what, you motherfucker? Are you fuckin' crazy?"

"Calm the fuck down, Odraye."

"You drop me in the shit, boy, I'll be the last fuckin' thing you see."

"You were seen on the street. He has witnesses, all three of us were seen. I told him you were there to help carry the refrigerator across the street. Just a guy Leotis knew. I didn't give him your name or any details," Butchie said, all in a rush to get it over with.

"You handled him?"

"I just told you. He was putty in my hands."

"Lyin' ass dog, you better not be shitting me on this."

"We're good."

For now but for how long? Butchie thought. He wouldn't take even odds on it lasting another twenty-four hours.

"You better be calling from a got-damn pay phone," Odraye said.

"You know how hard it is to find a payphone in this town—one that works?"

"If you're on your fuckin' cell phone—"

"I'm at a Dairy Queen on Belmont."

"Have an ice cream while you're there."

"Go fuck yourself."

CHAPTER 11

Butchie relocated the bags to his Jeep. No sense in tempting Odraye when he was away for more than an hour.

Delores Negrón owned a car. No big deal in the overall scheme of things, Butchie thought, except that it happened to be the same dented Toyota Odraye's amigo drove. He watched her leave the upstairs apartment. She was dressed for clubbing: tight, slutty Lycra skirt, bone-white blouse with a lot of cleavage and costume jewelry. Her platform shoes added three inches to her height.

She drove across town from Crescent to Belmont to Brockton High; she managed to hit all the red lights so that Butchie had an easy time staying in her wake. From Foster, she drove past the high school to Memorial Drive into Champion Park and pulled up near the Rocky Marciano statue. There, the pride of all red-blooded white Brocktonians stood twenty feet tall, frozen in glory with the punch that put "Jersey Joe" Walcott down in '52 extended toward infinity, although many would say Walcott was a tired old man by then.

The man who appeared from behind the statue and hopped into her car was a light-skinned black male wearing a Samuel B. Jackson-style beret that hung over half his face. Butchie would have recognized him without the cigarette.

Apparently, Delores didn't like smoking in her vehicle because the barely smoked cigarette came flying out the window as she made the roundabout to exit the park.

They stopped at a CVS and made a second stop on Belmont at Charlie's in the Stop-and-Shop Plaza. Diz came out with two Styrofoam cups in his hands. For the next fifteen minutes, they parked and drank. Butchie kept them in sight from the parking lot of the McDonald's across the street. He was too far away to see whether the conversation they had inside the car was animated but nothing looked out of the ordinary.

Delores started up the Toyota with a blue plume of burnt oil and they returned the route they had taken. When Delores pulled up in front of Brockton High to let Diz out, he decided to take a chance.

He followed him inside. Diz was helloing and high-fiving his way down the corridor. Butchie passed a big sign on an artist easel that said All Visitors Must Report to the Central Office. He could see a security guard and a metal detector beside a pair of tables fifteen feet ahead.

Any farther and he'd risk exposing himself to the guard; he hesitated, dropped to his knees and fussed with the lace of his work boot. When a group of three girls came abreast of him, he reached out and tapped the closest one on the shoulder.

"Miss, can you tell me who that gentleman is up ahead, the one in the black beret? He dropped his wallet outside."

"That's Mister Jelks," she said. "He teaches Spanish."

"I can give it to him for you," she said.

"That's all right," Butchie replied. "I'll give it to the security officer over there."

OK, Mister Jelks, a.k.a. Diz, let's find out why you're all up in my shit—slumming with a murderous thug and seeing a woman who cries rape.

Maurice Jelks was something of a public figure, lo and behold. The Brockton Public Library on Main was a hop-and-skip from the Rocky statue. A helpful librarian brought him an old newspaper photograph of Maurice receiving an award from the student body president as Teacher of the Year. The computer gave him Jelks's Facebook page, which was a whole lot of nothing, just self-promotion and goody-goody stuff a teacher would post. Especially a teacher who wanted to cultivate an image of being "selfless" and "dedicated," two words that kept popping up in posts whenever "Mr. Jelks" announced some Spanish Club event he was planning or posting photos of. No sign of the ever-present cigarette in any of the selfies.

The public records database showed the property Jelks owned, a modest bungalow, no garage, on Falconer. He used Google Earth to scan it from 360 degrees. Low-key, a manicured lawn, very middle-class. A black Navigator SUV sat in the driveway, but the photos looked to have been taken the past winter when snow was on the ground and a frost rimed the nearby roofs and hoods of cars. The satellite images might be six weeks or six months old.

Why borrow a clapped-out Toyota? Butchie wondered.

Odraye wasn't all that careful about covering his tracks. The garage door was jimmied; splinters and chunks of wood lay about the concrete floor of the garage. The loft ladder had been left down and every bundle of insulation had been pulled free between the joists and tossed aside. It was nothing more than he expected. The outlines of one large boot imprint created a kind of sooty collage on the door leading into the house. The door was cracked but it had held.

Three voicemails confirmed the vandal's identity.

"OK, you moved it," Odraye thundered, "but you sure as motherfuckin' shit better have it there for me to see when I come over."

"Where you at, motherfucker?"

"Butchie, I'm going to smash your fuckin' face in you don't call me back RIGHT FUCKING NOW YOU MOTHERFUCKER!"

Was it his old man or one of the nuns who used to talk about something called a Faustian bargain? Butchie couldn't recall but he knew it meant you were for sure screwed.

CHAPTER 12

Butchie sat alone in a back booth of the Dunkin' Donuts, pondering. It wasn't a word he had ever spoken aloud but it seemed appropriate under the circumstances. There was a lot to ponder. His jaw ached with every bite of the glazed donut. Thank God, Anthony was a wanna-be tough guy and not a real street fighter or professional boxer like Odraye. The duct tape on his hand must have wrapped up more than his knuckles. Butchie figured he'd put a few rings on his fingers. Odraye was out there looking for him right now, pissed as all hell because he'd relocated the money, as if he'd even see the money if the situation had been reversed. Only the fact Odraye was either jugged or in transit, sleeping on couches and hanging out with the mysterious Maurice Jelks, kept him from booking town with all the swag and leaving Butchie behind. Probably in the same shape as Leotis with a massive dent in his head and his brains in his nasal passage. Butchie had no trouble remembering the arc of the sledgehammer coming down on Leotis's head followed by that sound like a melon being dropped from a third-story window to the sidewalk.

"Pound-for-pound, who was the better fighter?"

Fuck me. Dominic Hoyt, big as life. . . how did a man that size enter a room silent as a cat and creep up on him like this?

"Mister Hoyt."

"Call me Dom. I'll call you Butchie," Hoyt said. His grin wasn't as big as the Cheshire Cat's on the Disney channel but close to it.

"You found me."

"That implies I was looking for you."

"Were you?"

"Can't a fella just be a tourist and enjoy the sights of your fair town? I mean this place, Brockton, it has a lot of history. It used to be famous for shoes, right?"

"That's right, a long time ago."

"But I don't see any factories making shoes, yet everybody's gotta have a pair on, am I right?"

"So maybe you should complain to the Chamber of Commerce, not me," Butchie said.

"So I return to my original question. Pound-for-pound. Marciano or Hagler?"

"Apples and oranges," Butchie said. "Different times, different weight classes."

"But Marciano, he finished—what? Forty-nine and zero. Undefeated. An unblemished record, as they say."

Butchie remembered a fight breaking out in the Fratellanza Club between a couple guys over whether the Rock's unblemished record was, in fact, unblemished. The one guy claimed Marciano's first fight was an unrecorded bout he lost shortly after turning pro under a fake name.

"That's true," Butchie said. "Where are we going with this?"

"Oh, just shooting the shit, a couple guys having a pleasant conversation about your hometown heroes. You like it here, Butchie? You like living in Brockton?"

"It's home."

"That isn't what I asked you," Hoyt replied.

The grin came back, widened a bit. One of Butchie's high school classmates had a facial tic, got the nickname "Blinky" for it. Butchie thought of Hoyt's cat-grin appearing and disappearing like the cat. When he first dated Denise DiGiacomo, they sat on the couch with her little nephew watching Alice in Wonderland. Anthony and both Neecie's parents sat around the room talking, pretending to watch the cartoon, too, but they were really watching him. Neecie's thigh rubbed his, her tangy perfume, it all became too much, and though he watched the episode between Alice and the Cat, the blood was rushing south like a broken dam and he was afraid they'd all spot his excitement. Five months into their dating, Neecie told him she knew all along he was hiding an erection.

"What do you want me to say, Dom? It's an armpit of a town and I can't wait to blow the dust of it off my shoes?"

"Shoes, that's funny. We were just talking about shoes. I swung by the Rocky Marciano statue while I was out cruising the streets."

"Looking for a donut?"

"Something like that," Hoyt replied. "I see that long arm…"

Hoyt covered up like a boxer, swaying like a cobra sensing danger, then, assuming the famous peek-a-boo style of Floyd Patterson, he shot a couple jabs across the table at Butchie. Hoyt's right stopped just short of Butchie's nose. Close enough for him to see the crisscross of tiny white scars across the knuckles. Hoyt wouldn't be the type to wrap his hands. He wouldn't need rings.

"I heard you were in the Army," Butchie said.

Hoyt belly-laughed. A few heads swiveled their way.

"Butchie, I'm impressed! You were investigating me." He looked serious again. "You got a license in this state to do that, Parmenter?" Another big laugh.

"Just heard it from a friend."

"A friend," Hoyt repeated. "You heard it through the grapevine." Hoyt sang a few words of the Motown song badly off-key. "A different Marvin, Marvin Gaye. Gladys Knight and the Pips, too."

"I'm impressed, Dominic. A soldier, a shamus, a boxing fan, and an expert on popular culture, too. You're a real Renaissance man."

"Yeah, that's me," Hoyt said, and that crooked smile came back and went away just as fast.

"Here's something else I know. Rocky Marciano, your big hometown hero in this shitheap of a city, was a miser. He never spent a dime. He kept all his cash in paper bags just like old Mrs. Bello."

"I heard he used to do that," Butchie said. "Maybe he didn't trust banks, either."

"That's an interesting word, Butchie. Trust. Who do you trust? I know what I trust, and it isn't you, my friend. Enjoy your donuts while you can, shithead."

Hoyt brought out a business card and skimmed it across the table. It hit Butchie's coffee mug and flipped over.

"It's my business card," Hoyt said. "You asked me for one when we met. There it is. My cell number is on it."

Butchie said nothing. He watched Hoyt get out of the booth and stand up. For a man his size, he moved gracefully. Butchie thought of Neecie's cat Jezebel, a pampered and overfed animal that was jealous of his attention for her owner.

"You don't think so right now," Hoyt added. "But you're going to want to talk to me one of these days."

"Why would you think that, Mister Hoyt?"

"Because I can prevent bad accidents from happening."

"What sort of bad accident?"

"The kind that can get the yellow shit stomped out of you just crossing the street."

Butchie remembered something about the Cheshire Cat. It told Alice a dog growled when it was angry and wagged its tail when it was pleased. Now I growl when I'm pleased and wag my tail when I'm angry. The point wasn't lost on Alice or Butchie: Therefore, I'm mad.

He expected to see the banged-up white Toyota sitting in his parking spot, a long brown arm hanging out the window with a cigarette in its fingers. Instead, it was Neecie's maroon Honda Civic.

He could see her eyes studying the rearview as he pulled up.

She exited the car and came toward him. "Butchie."

"Hey, Neecie."

"I'm sorry. I heard what my stupid brother did, the sfaccimme."

Calling Anthony a "sperm" was one of her many favorite

expressions of contempt for him besides stronzo, "asshole," and dumb stroons, "shit." His was any of a half-dozen variations for "pussy." Like any brother and sister growing up in a large Italian family, the cussing and arguing between them was constant and vigorous.

She cupped his chin in her hand and turned him this way and that like a jeweler looking for a flaw in a facet.

Butchie gently pulled her wrist away. "It's nothing."

"Don't look like nothing, Butchie. It's all swollen and purple under there."

"Forget it, Denise."

"Denise? That means you're pissed off at me, too."

"Honestly, I'm just having a bad day—week," Butchie replied; Life, he could have said.

He attempted to walk past her, but she chest-bumped him like one con bracing another in the yard.

"He can be a real sta'nod, Butchie, I know that."

"It's all right, no big deal," Butchie said. He placed his hands on her shoulders and attempted to move her out of his way. "Look, I'm not mad at you. I'm not mad at Anthony. He needs to find better friends to hang with."

As if I'm in any position to give advice on that subject.

"You think I haven't told him that? It's all I hear around the house," she said. "Those Pagans or Banditos or whatever the hell they are will get him in big trouble one of these days."

"Come on in. I want to talk to you about something."

"Butchie, I don't want to talk about us," she said.

"No, not us," he said. "Something else. I just want to talk to somebody I trust."

Trust, Hoyt's word to him that morning.

"Go to the cops," Neecie told him. "Right now."

"I can't," Butchie said. "I waited too long."

"Tell them you were afraid of this Suggs guy. You thought if you didn't go along with it—the sledgehammer party—he was going to do you next."

"What about the money?"

"Return it."

"Just like that, Neecie? I lied all over the place. I'm in too deep now."

Her disgust was all too evident. Butchie knew the signs by heart. The wrinkling of her nose while he sputtered one lame explanation or excuse after the other for the last fifteen minutes was the most telling; it said I smell excrement better than anything. He didn't even want to think about what she'd say if he mentioned Delores Negrón. Separated or not, she expected celibacy until he was dropped into his lonely grave. Having casual sex with a woman was bad enough, not to mention the rape allegation. Still, she didn't bolt from his living room when he told her about Leotis Marsten's murder.

"Jeez, the paper didn't have shit about it. It just said he was found dead," she said.

"The cops like to keep things back. They trip up suspects that way," he said. Mr. Forensics now.

"You say this other guy, the private eye hired by the Bellos. He knows?"

"He knows."

"Butchie, you better get a lawyer."

"I can't afford one, Neecie."

"I'll give you the money," she said. "I'll loan you the money."

"No."

"Then it's your funeral, Butchie, and I can't do nothing for you."

"You already did," Butchie said.

"What?"

"You listened to me. I was gonna bust apart if I didn't tell somebody what all the shit was raining down on me these last few days. It's been a nightmare."

"Yeah, well, it's only gonna get worse."

"You'll come visit me in prison?"

"Va'fa'un culo."

She slammed the door behind her.

That expression didn't need a translation; he knew that one

too well.

The caller's voice was somebody he didn't recognize.

"Why do you want to help me?" Butchie asked the caller. The voice was male, twenties to thirties, most likely, but indistinct as far as race.

"Because, like, she burned a friend of mine this way coupla years ago. The guy had more trouble after it, even when the cops proved there was no assault. I mean, man, she ruined the guy's life. He was paying a lawyer, lost his job over it. Half the town didn't—still doesn't believe him."

"Where was this?" Butchie asked the voice.

"Boston. Three years ago."

"I know people in Boston," Butchie said. "Can you give me something more specific?"

"Hey, you think I'm jerking you off? I'm just trying to help you out here. Who knows how many guys she's done this to? Probably don't even know about the ones who paid her off just to shut her up."

"I still want to know some names and places," Butchie said.

"How about you meet my friend? Will that do? He can tell you in person how she scammed him."

"Where in Boston?"

"Boston? Naw, man, here in Brockton. He left town right after the D.A. refused to prosecute. They told him his case was stetted, if that means anything to you. He's got a new life here, a good job in IT, married and kids. He's happy."

"If it comes to it," Butchie asked, "will he sign a statement or testify?"

"That, now, I can't say. He might not want his wife to know about the hell she put him through. Look, I'll do this much. I'll call him tonight. If he agrees, he can meet you somewhere and you two can discuss it between you. This is as far as I'm going with it," the voice said.

The man on the other end sounded serious, reasonable, articulate. None of the chopped-up, slangy, truncated speech of the usual run-of-the-mill Brocktonian he encountered on the job or about town.

Around one-fifteen, Butchie still hadn't heard from Odraye. He kept parting the sheers in front of the window every time a car pulled into the complex. The same insouciant tomcat with glittering green-gold eyes walked across the lot with its tail snubbed and one mangled ear.

He was tying off the last of his homemade warning system—washed steel cans tied with fishing line and rigged to the back door and all the windows—when his cell rang on the bedside table.

"He'll meet you in the Denny's off Twenty-Four in the Westgate Mall. You know where that is?"

"I know it."

"Forty, fifty minutes, he said. Come alone. He don't want a crowd there. All this is embarrassing, and he wants to put it behind him. He's doing me a favor, not you. Got it?"

"Tell him I'm on my way," Butchie said and thumbed off the connection.

He don't want. . . The familiar colloquialism the voice's first grammar slip. Or am I just being paranoid?

The girl waiting on him had pink hair with blue streaks. She kept forgetting the little creamers for the coffee. He checked his watch. An hour and seven minutes since the phone call. The guy wasn't coming. Butchie put four dollars on the table, hesitated and took one bill back; she didn't deserve four bucks for the shitty service.

The lot had more cars than people inside the restaurant, a curiosity about twenty-four-hour places he'd often wondered about. Where were they? They weren't all working in the kitchen washing dishes for six customers.

He'd just unlocked his car and smelled cigarette smoke when hard metal flicked his left ear.

"Don't fuckin' turn around," the phone voice said. "Get in—passenger seat. Quick!"

Butchie hoisted himself up and moved over to the passenger seat.

Maurice Jelks slipped into the driver's seat.

"Give me the keys."

Butchie handed them over.

Jelks rested a snub-nosed revolver against his chest, the barrel pointing at Butchie's ribs, and halted midway before inserting the key in the ignition. He stared.

"What the fuck—"

"What's wrong, Jelks? Can't drive stick?"

Jelks sat back against the seat.

"No, God damn it. Why the fuck they still make these things?"

"You should have thought it out better," Butchie said.

"All right, fuck it. We talk right here. Odraye wants his share of the money, and how do you know my name?"

"Why isn't Odraye asking me for it, Diz—or should I call you Maurice?"

"I'll ask the questions," Jelks said. "You miss the fact I'm holding the gun? I'll blow a fuckin' hole through you."

"That's a big gun, but I don't think it could actually do that."

Butchie wasn't sure why he felt like taunting the man.

"No, but the ammo inside it can," Jelks snapped. "You know what a hollow point can do to human flesh? No pass-through. It'll fragment inside you and won't even break the window. I was you, I'd shut the fuck up and answer my question."

"Your DNA is all over this car now, Maurice. I keep a log in writing and on my computer. Your name features prominently so—"

"So shut the fuck up, Parmenter, and tell me where the goddamned money's hidden. Odraye, he's got even less patience than I do."

"OK, I'll tell you," Butchie said.

"No, shithead, you're going to show me," Jelks replied.

Jelks, tall but nimble, held the barrel against Butchie's head and they exited the passenger side door like a pair of Siamese twins. The sodium arc lights from the highway cast an orange glow over everything. Light traffic on the nearby highway, the early risers still tucked into bed, maybe the bakers and night maintenance people still active. As they rounded the back of the Wrangler, Butchie looked toward the Denny's windows and saw a pair of heads in a booth. They didn't look his way.

"Get your dago ass in the fucking seat and stop dawdling," Jelks demanded. He jabbed the barrel hard into Butchie's back.

"That how you talk to your Spanish students when they're late for class?"

"You already proved you know who I am," Jelks said. "Don't push your luck. I'm gonna scoot over you now. Keep very still. This gun will be pressed against your face the whole time. You make a sudden move—Blam! You hear me?"

Come down to it, Butchie realized, he wouldn't be all that broken up about losing his share of the money. Nothing good had happened since that day in Bello's store. The absurdity of this man, about six-two, trying to squeeze his body over him in the tight confines of his Jeep. When Jelks reached with one hand for the head rest to twist himself around, the gun barrel slipped away from Butchie's face and he instinctively slammed his head into Jelks's face.

Jelks tried to bring the gun up, but his wrist slammed into the steering wheel and it flew out of his hand. Butchie drew back a fist to throw a punch but it was like fighting inside a closet. He used a forearm to throw off Jelks and lever him into the passenger seat. Blood from Jelks's nose flew all around them like a lawn sprinkler. Butchie slammed his hand against the door latch and jumped out to the pavement. Jelks slithered after him and wound up on top of Butchie on the asphalt. They struggled, locked in an embrace, both men fearing the other had the weapon.

Butchie couldn't see who was standing a few feet from them but he noted work boots and heard a man's voice just behind them: "Check this shit out, Lou. Coupla fags having a lover's quarrel."

Butchie felt the weight removed from his chest. He pushed

himself up and rolled away, fearing a shot from Jelks's gun—but there was nobody there. The two men who'd observed them were walking toward a utility van. Jelks was nowhere in sight. He looked around for the dirty white Toyota and saw nothing but the same vehicles in the lot. One of the workmen, seeing Butchie staggering around, bloodied, sneered: "Your boyfriend took off, blowboy. He's long gone." Butchie heard the other man snort something about "fucking homos."

He staggered back to his Jeep, astounded from the close call. His hands were shaking. His pocket flap was ripped loose and hung down like a tongue. Oily grime smeared streaks down both pant legs when Jelks landed on him and he had a bad road rash on one elbow. But he was alive, no bullet holes, thank God. Why risk his life to headbutt a guy with a gun inches from his face? It was beyond stupid. Butchie wondered if his psyche was acting up, trying to kill him. Some underground river of Catholic guilt must have eaten its way into his subconscious.

He found the gun, a Smith & Wesson five-shot Bodyguard, beneath the driver's seat. The black butt of the gun lying in plain sight. Butchie opened the drum just to see if Jelks had been telling the truth about the load. He popped a couple rounds into his hand. Winchester PDX1 was written around the cartridge rim and the copper jackets suggested Jelks didn't exaggerate. With all the school shootings going on, all the teachers in America were arming themselves on the sly, packing firepower in case theirs was the next place to go up. He thought of his tiny Beretta back home in the drawer. He not only didn't bring that to a gun fight, he didn't even bring a knife.

I'm way, way out of my depth, Butchie thought.

Traffic was picking up and the sky was lightening just enough to remove the metallic glint from the car hoods and the fixtures of rooftops. Commercial signage with their LED programmable lights looked less urgent in the gauzy pre-dawn gray light. Gulls screeched overhead, en route to restaurant parking lots for the food scraps left behind in discarded wrappers or chucked out of car windows. Another day coming, Butchie realized. At least he wasn't lying prone on the ground with paramedics trying to staunch the massive wound channel of a fragmentation round. He should consider himself lucky for that much absolution.

It's just a reprieve, Butchie thought. Now that Odraye Suggs, Delores Negrón, and Maurice Jelks had formed a coalition to move against him, he'd have to prepare for them next time as well as the tag-team of Hoyt and Det. Forshey. A new day, his father used to say, meant a new beginning. He thought of a better expression from Neecie's half-senile grandfather brought over from Italy, whose endless grinding of his American dentures was a source of amusement for the younger siblings in her family. Butchie asked Neecie what he was mumbling all the time and she repeated it: "Che cazzo è?" It means, "What the fuck is this?"

"Sorry I asked," Butchie remembered saying. When they started having sex, these were the first words he said to her, enraptured by the animal lust consummated on her bed.

Now he stood alone and looked at a gull circling a discarded cigarette butt before getting up the nerve to dash for it and clamp it in his bill and take off. A second later, it dropped the butt near Butchie's feet. "I hear you, pal," Butchie said, alone in the somber light spreading around the lot. "Che cazzo è? My sentiments exactly."

"She say why?"

"Not to me," Det. Forshey said. "Called the precinct this morning, talked to my L.T., and said she was no longer interested in charging you with rape. You're a lucky man, Parmenter."

Forshey seemed relaxed, less tense than on his first visit, but Butchie didn't trust him. Yet the news about Delores was good. He didn't need that hanging over his head with all the rest of it going on.

"We're looking for the man who was with you that day," Forshey said. "Maybe you can help. Say, this coffee's good, much better than the swill we drink at the stationhouse. Is it a special brand?"

"You mean some bean that only grows on the side of a hill in East Africa and gets picked by moonlight?"

"Yeah, special like that, smart ass."

"I don't know," Butchie said. "I buy whatever's on sale. I just got a Keurig."

"I been thinking about buying one of those. For the house, I mean, not the station. Shit, man, those guys will drink lukewarm battery acid and not know the difference. Me, I like good coffee."

"Sorry, Detective, I can't help. I saw the guy with Marsten like I told you. He just stood in the background. I did my inspection and took off. I never even got a good look at him except that he was big."

"Big, yes, I'll say. He's a boxer from around here, name's Odraye Suggs," Forshey said.

"Yeah?"

"Yeah. According to one of the detectives at the station, this Suggs is around six-four, goes about two-eighty. Can't box worth a piss. My guy follows the sport. 'He'd be something in the ring if he knew how to throw a combination' is what he tells me."

He knows how to swing a friggin' sledge, Butchie thought. No trouble there. And as for combinations, that one punch to the jaw was sufficient unto the day. . .

"I don't follow much boxing," Butchie said. "Get you a refill?"

"No, thanks, I'm good. Got to run," Forshey said.

He stood up and stretched. He handed Butchie the mug but let his grip on the handle linger.

"One thing," Forshey said, patting his pocket for his keys.

"What's that?"

"I read your report, the inspection. Pretty detailed, all that jazz about wiring and plumbing, footers. Descriptions of the water damage and the holes in every room. Good eye for detail. But you never mentioned the refrigerator in your inventory."

"I don't remember what I wrote. Too many places came and went since then."

"Sure, Butchie. Like Odraye Suggs standing right beside you on the street, big enough to eat apples off your head, a local palooka who helps Marsten tote some refrigerator across the street.

"Guy never said who he was and I don't follow boxing."

"You don't follow much boxing," Forshey repeated, nodding. "What about your other visit, the one last Friday when Marsten got his head stove in. Did you mention Marsten or the big guy, Odraye Suggs, in it?"

"That wasn't a report," Butchie said. "I sometimes add an auxiliary report to the first when conditions change. Not that time."

"Conditions changed for Marsten, though. Guy used to have a functioning head and a complete brain before blunt force trauma turned half of it into scrambled eggs."

"Look, I was long gone by then," Butchie said.

"That's right," the cop said, "I remember you said that."

Forshey left without another word. Butchie watched him get into an unmarked car, a beige sedan, something vice cops liked to use on stakeout; like a big cat in the Serengeti grass, it blended in. Butchie wondered if he'd just exchanged Jelks's tail for another.

He locked the door and headed for the cupboard where he kept the expensive Scotch malt.

Fuck me, he knows everything, Butchie thought, everything.

It was midday, and he hadn't slept yet. It wasn't the aftereffects of the adrenalin from the fight in the parking lot so much as the fear that Odraye would show up in a rage and he'd have to hold him off with his peashooter. He was lucky that Forshey caught him just as he'd cleaned up in the shower and didn't look much worse for wear. He was thinking of trading up, getting something that held manstopper rounds, if any such ammo existed.

Brockton wasn't Boston, not yet, but the murders reported in the Globe and Channel 5 were eye-opening. Just last week one gangbanger shot another fourteen times and the guy lived—at least for the four blocks he was able to run away until he bled out. Unless he hit Odraye in the brain, spine, or blew out an aorta with his first shot, he wasn't sure he'd get a second one. Even the Beretta's rounds would penetrate drywall, however. He hadn't been to the gun range in 8 or 9 months and he was no marksman. His complex was full of families with kids. God, he didn't need anything else on his conscience besides Leotis.

The trouble, Butchie knew, was he still wanted to keep the money—some of it, anyhow, if not his full share. More and more, he was feeling he'd "earned" it through the trauma of what happened. It was the Bello family's money; he knew that. But it wouldn't penetrate deep enough into his thinking. Not greed so much as stubbornness. The money could buy him a new start. He knew he was slipping into the mire, and it wouldn't be all that long before Asaro got rid of him even if he survived his hearing tomorrow morning, which was doubtful. The kickbacks, the bribes, the old take-the-money-don't-rock-the-boat was wearing him down. He was no crusader and he damn sure wasn't a hero. Too much corruption all around, and he just wanted out.

Why else play the cat-and-mouse with Forshey? He could blurt out the whole sordid catastrophe involving Odraye, Jelks, and Negrón, get it over with, and hold out his wrists for the cuffs.

I can't do that—sorry everybody, Butchie said to his empty room. It was as if all the ghosts of his past had surrounded him, crowding around waiting for him to do the right thing. His dad and mom, most of all, their faces etched with grief. Neecie shaking her head in dismay. All his old teachers, the nuns and priests of his parish. If he closed his eyes, he could glimpse old bald Fr. Guido Montesanti, aghast behind the latticed screen in the confessional box at Butchie's admission—yet again—of another nightly marathon masturbation session. "Now, this, you—you stroons! Che cavollo, what are you doing to your immortal soul?" Even the Bellos, whom he'd never met, were back there lurking, horrified at what their mother's money had caused, their inheritance in the hands of two remorseless thugs.

Butchie decided it was time to find Odraye and get this hideous business done, gone, and out of his life for good. He went into the bedroom and pulled a garbage bag of money from under it. He opened the drawer and took out the Beretta. He had no intention of provoking Suggs. He'd toss him the money, wish him luck, and get out of there as fast as he could. Every man for himself from now on.

That was the plan. What was it "Iron" Mike Tyson used to say about a plan? Everyone's got one until you get hit in the face.

Butchie parked down the block. He could still see her white Toyota parked in front of the house. Maybe a catnap to smooth his ragged nerves. His right eyeball itched; he rubbed the socket until it squeaked.

An hour later, Butchie was drifting into a pleasant daydream: a mojito in one hand, wading near the shoreline while waves lap against his bare legs. A pair of giggling girls walk past him, their feet scrunching in the wet sand and the muscles of their legs flexing. They're tanned and curvy in their bright bikinis. He enjoys watching them, in no mood to do anything but enjoy the surf, the sun, and the gorgeous turquoise water stretching out toward the horizon and another golden sunset. . .

Jelks came out of her apartment. Even from this distance, Butchie could see the huge bandage across the bridge of his nose. He had raccoon eyes and wore a baseball cap and a hoodie sweatshirt with Boston U embossed across the front.

Playing hooky today, Mister Jelks?

Jelks took the steps two at a time and started walking down the block where Butchie parked between a couple big SUVs.

Butchie hunkered down in his seat and kept his eye on the sideview mirror. It seemed for a moment Jelks was striding right at him, coming down the sidewalk. Jelks shaded his eyes, making a tent against the glare of the sun. Then he loped off in another direction. Butchie relaxed his grip on the Beretta tucked into his belt.

Butchie wanted to catch Delores fast, let her think it was Jelks coming right back. Once the Toyota exited the lot, he was out of the Jeep and moving fast toward the stairs.

Three quick raps.

No chain lock this time. She opened the door and saw who it was, attempted to slam it on his leg. She fumbled with the chain but Butchie already had a purchase with his thigh and wedged the door open, pushing her backward.

"Delores, I just want to talk."

She had her cell in her hand. Butchie motioned with his hands up, palms out.

"Please don't call," he said. "I just want a few words with you. I'm not upset, see, and I won't hurt you. A short talk is all and then I'll go away forever."

She hesitated. Butchie willed her thumb away from the 9 button he knew she'd just pressed. She looked at him, her face blank, expressionless, and thumbed the 1.

"Please," he said again.

She set the phone on the counter. "What do you want?"

"Did Maurice Jelks—the guy who just left this apartment—so you know I know, did he set me up? Was it his idea or Odraye Suggs' to have you call the cops on me?"

"Mo's idea but Odraye went along with it. They thought if you got into trouble, Odraye would be able to get the money you stole from him. Keep you busy or keep you in jail."

"I didn't—never mind that now. How did Maurice Jelks know you and I were involved?"

Butchie surprised himself with the word choice. Three people were trying to destroy him, and he's standing there with one of them pussyfooting around. Jesus, shit, fuck.

"They was both here drinking one night. Mo come over for

his weed like he always do. Odraye keeps the high schools supplied. Sells them this shit he calls his 'Panama Gold.'"

Butchie remembered Nino's words in the bar. . . They call him 'The Wild Panamanian.'

"I thought he was a prizefighter?"

"He only fight, like, once a year. He don't make any money boxing," Delores said. "The Bachelor was on. Odraye's cussing out some guy who screwed him over. He say the guy was a housing inspector, and I mention this place got inspected. One thing and another, yadda-yadda, and they figure, like, you was the guy ripped off Odraye."

"You always screw your housing inspectors, Delores? Every swinging dick who gets called in?"

"Fuck you, you fuck!"

"Sorry. That was stupid. I didn't mean it," Butchie replied.

"Quinnel say, he said he'd give me two months free if I done you. I got three kids I'm tryin' to get out of Child Services, man! You think it's easy being a single mother, cabrón?"

"I'm sorry about your kids, Delores. But these guys are trying to kill me."

"Then you better give that money back, ladrón. You call me a whore but you a fuckin' thief!"

Outside on the landing, he gripped the iron stairwell and stared off in the distance. Quinnel had jury-rigged it to the house. If you hopped from one foot to the other, the whole thing shook and threatened to come down like a house of cards. He never gave any thought whether a mother and her three kids would be safe on it when he was banging Delores inside. When did it start to go bad and why didn't I try to stop it? Butchie wondered. Little by little, you lose your bearings and you forget what everybody tried to teach you about doing the right thing when you were a kid.

Butchie figured he had some soul-searching coming. Just not now. Too much was going on. He stopped believing in the supernatural before he was out of his teens, yet here he was, a man in his thirties counting the ghosts of his past and not liking the tally.

CHAPTER 13

It was the shortest hearing possible. Asaro looked smug. He'd even worn a suit for the occasion.

He sat between a ward member of city council, the Housing Planning Commissioner, the Brockton Mayor's personal assistant, and a couple people who were introduced to Butchie as being department heads with triple-word civil service titles, but he forgot them as soon as they were seated around the conference table.

They even had a bailiff from the courthouse in case Butchie went postal—or he guessed that was the guy's purpose for looking so glum sitting off by himself and ignored.

Even Asaro called him "Mister Parmenter," a bizarre courtesy for the others in the room. The proceedings were formally described as a disciplinary hearing, which was some relief to Butchie.

He kept waiting to hear Leotis Marsten's name mentioned, but it never happened. Asaro took over and did most of the talking. Butchie watched him take out a printout and a pair of glasses from his suitcoat pocket, unfold the paper, put on the glasses, and begin reading the list of Butchie's crimes and misdemeanors. It amounted to a dozen infractions of petty rules regarding "use of city vehicles," "insubordination" ("Mister Parmenter told me to kiss his ass, quote, on March Fourteenth of last year when I rebuked him for failing to observe city ordinance one-one-three, which requires all employees. . .")

To Butchie, it sounded no worse than littering during a hurricane. If he or any other civil employee of the great city of Brockton actually followed the rules, the city would collapse into chaos. You couldn't keep track of everything without toting around a three-ring binder full of regulations.

When Asaro attempted to bring in the allegation of Delores Negrón, it was quickly quashed by the city solicitor. She was the last one to arrive and apologized for being late to the meeting.

"I think the committee should at least hear the charge," Asaro replied.

She was firm. "Absolutely not, Dan. An unsubstantiated charge like that is mere hearsay and only pollutes the proceedings."

Butchie loved the phrase. . . pollutes the proceedings. It was a woman who rose to his defense. She might have saved his job with that one stroke.

When it came his time to talk, Butchie thanked the members for convening in his behalf, regretted it was necessary, and began to refute the "charges" against him—all but the insubordination.

"I have no excuse for that," he told them. "I work closely with Dan. I mean, Mister Asaro, and we often speak informally and casually to each other."

"Do you routinely make obscene suggestions like that, as Mister Asaro has indicated?"

"No, I don't. Sure, sometimes I lose my temper. Like that incident he mentioned when it was minus ten degrees and I'm running into and out of derelict buildings with no heat all day, and Dan—Mister Asaro here—orders me to go back out to inspect a place some other inspector had fu—screwed up in his own report."

Butchie couldn't read their faces, but he knew what a defendant in court had to feel like. All stone faces except for Asaro who glowered at him whenever their glances locked and Ms. Hemmings, the solicitor. She seemed nice and didn't cut her eyes away if he happened to look her way.

"We'll meet separately, Mister Parmenter," the chair said as the meeting wound up. He was one of the department heads with a mysterious title. "We will get back to you as soon as possible. Meanwhile, we're going to let Superintendent Asaro's disciplinary action stand. You are to remain suspended with pay. Pending our decision, you will have access to an appeal through the city manager's office and a form will be provided you with names and numbers from Human Resources. Thank you, everybody."

Ms. Hemmings gave him a quick smile on her way past. "Good luck," she said.

A no-decision. Butchie was OK with it under the circumstances. He'd expected a kangaroo court. Despite all the bureaucratic mumbo-jumbo and ordinance this-and-that of the city code, Asaro sounded hostile and small-minded. He didn't sound like Employee of the Month, but he was far short of the Nazi war criminal Asaro had tried to paint him to the others. He was afraid that Det. Forshey's or Hoyt's names would be brought up at some point in Asaro's list, but it didn't happen. He still had money coming in. He was on the verge of visiting his parents to ask for a loan.

But at least this much was out of the way and he could concentrate on his next move. He had one big fish to fry and it was named Odraye Suggs. Old Fr. Montesanti liked to nip the altar wine, or so the rumor went, and whenever he had a chance, he resorted to his favorite sermon. Butchie, an altar boy in those days, got a kick out of seeing the old priest weave around the altar, buzzed on the wine or whatever he'd imbibed before mass in the sacristy. Begowned in his beautiful satin priest robes, he'd skip like a goat from one end of the altar to the other, always a half-step from taking a tumble. But get him onto the subject of the "Day of Judgment," and he was masterful at the lectern during the sermon. He thundered and slapped one hand against the other simulating the lightning claps of God's wrath. "Dies Irae," he roared in his magnificent basso-profundo voice. "That Day of Judgment is coming for you all!"

Butchie's stomach churned at the memory. He was surrounded by a couple pairs of demons whispering in his ear:

Odraye and Jelks on one shoulder and Forshey and Hoyt in the other.

But did he really have a choice? His dies irae was barreling down on his ass no matter how ready or unready he was for it.

CHAPTER 14

"Bool-shit!"

"It's the truth," Butchie said. "I just left the meeting. You want to talk, we'll talk. But I ain't gonna meet you in another goddamned dark parking lot at midnight so your bitch can jump me again."

"What the fuck are you talking about?" Odraye demanded.

"Don't waste my time, Odraye. I swear to God, I'll mail your share and mine both to the cops."

"Wait, wait! Hold on, Butchie! What the fuck's the matter with you, boy?"

"Nothing. I'm being stalked by a high-school teacher and a psycho loon who smashes people's heads in on a whim. Nothing at all's the matter with me."

"OK, OK, take a breath. Calm the fuck down," Odraye said.

Mr. Voice of Reason now, Butchie thought.

"I got me a little problem with Five-O at the moment," Odraye said. "I can't be out there runnin' the streets all damn day lookin' for you. Diz, he my fren' and he agree to help me out. Maybe he got carried away a bit."

"That's a funny way to describe attempted kidnapping," Butchie said.

"I tole him, just bring Butchie here—that's all, man. I didn't know he was going to pull a gat on you."

"You promise him my share? Look, don't waste any more time denying it. I want to get you the fuck out of my life right now," Butchie said. "I'll bring you your half of the money. Just tell me where to meet you."

"What about the—you know, exchange? What about all that shit's no good to spend right now?"

"That's not my problem," Butchie said. "I'm giving it back. I'm sending it to the Bello family. You keep your half. Just leave me out of it."

"Whoa, now, Butchie, let's think this through for a minute. My half of the money is no fucking good to me if your half is going to them people."

"What do you want from me?"

Oh shit. The light bulb just went off in Butchie's head. He was so entangled in the mess he helped create he never thought until this moment there was anything but greed behind Odraye's twists and turns. It wasn't just his share of the money now. He, Butchie, was a witness to murder. Odraye had set him up with Delores and her high-school teacher for more than his access to the Bello store: Odraye wanted him gone, as in dead gone.

"You know something, Odraye?"

"What's that, Butchie?"

"You can kiss my ass."

"You wop Motherfu—"

Butchie clicked him off. He noticed his hands shaking again. Nervous tremors rippled up and down his spine. He was a controlled mess. Barely. Delores hadn't told him everything. What she held back was the real reason she called off the rape charge. Odraye wanted him dead. She'd get his share, whatever portion Diz let her have, and she'd get her kids back. He guessed that was her incentive. As for Mister Maurice Jelks, the popular high-school teacher, his salary was probably better than Butchie's so it had to be a big enough bribe to get him to throw in with the likes of Odraye Suggs. From dope business to Murder Inc. in one step. Odraye wanted someone with enough class and smarts to do what Butchie proposed to do—that is, exchange the money without alerting half the US government's law-enforcement agencies as well as the Bello family clamoring for it through their proxy, one Dominic Hoyt, ex-military and current private eye.

Butchie had never considered himself a bigot in his entire life. He always took people straight on, not by their skin color. But had he short-changed Odraye on brains because he was not only a black street thug but a boxer?

He scrolled Nino Frabutt's number from the directory.

"Nino."

"That you, Butchie? Shit, I just woke up. Tied one on last night—"

"Nino, did Odraye Suggs, the boxer, did he put you up to introducing us?"

"Hell, I can't remember."

"Think, Nino, it's important."

"Coulda been like that—yeah. I was at that shitkicker bar you like so much, the biker's joint where Anthony hangs out. By the way, he's looking for youse, too."

"Forget him, he found me. Go on, tell me about Suggs."

"I thought it was strange, you know? Black dude his size in a biker joint. I thought maybe he was there looking for trouble. You know what it's like nowadays with all this Black-Lives-Matter horseshit and—"

"Nino, Jumping Jesus, will you focus? Suggs. I want to hear how you and him met up."

"Christ Almighty, give me a chance to think, you guinea putz. I told you I hung on one, didn't I? So I think, yeah, he came up to me, we started chatting about the Sox or some shit. He asked me, he said he needed a housing inspector, some guy he could trust to do a little job for him. What? What did you say?"

"Nothing. Go on. What did you say?"

"I said I know a guy. My friend Butchie Parmenter. He'll take care of you."

"Thanks, Nino, I gotta go."

"Hey, wait. Another guy was asking for you last night. Not Odraye. Tall, slender, light-skinned. Said he got into a fight. Looked like a fuckin raccoon, two black eyes, skin under 'em all yellow and purple like a spoiled banana. You know him?'"

"I know him. Thanks, Nino."

Shit on a fucking shingle. What a fool I am, Butchie realized. Looking for me all that time, looking for a guy on the take, a patsy he could use. Somebody he could use and throw away like Kleenex. . .

Butchie shivered suddenly despite the heat bearing down on him. It was going into a heat wave, the radio in his Jeep said. Neecie always said somebody walked on her grave whenever she got the chills like that. It was a flashback to the store, standing there, catching that blur of the sledge being brought down on Leotis that caused it. Something else, too: Odraye had already marked him as expendable. But he didn't kill Butchie then and there, and he could have just as easily as Leotis. Maybe he thought I was still useful, somebody to control until he could discard me for good.

Butchie had questions. The trouble was, he knew, the answers were coming to him so late he might never get a chance to know what, if any, future he had left.

"Neighbors called the cops," Hoyt said. "They thought you were throwing a wild party or something."

Butchie ignored him and kept walking toward his steps. One police officer stood on the steps talking to one half-leaning inside. The front door had been kicked off the hinges and the glass shattered.

Hoyt followed on his heels.

"Butchie, I think you've been keeping secrets from me."

"Leave me alone, Hoyt."

"Are you the resident?"

This from the cop on the steps.

"Yes, I live here. My name's Parmenter."

"Does he live here with you," the cop asked, gesturing behind him to Hoyt, standing there with that irritating grin on his mug.

"No, sir," Hoyt interjected before Butchie could speak. "I'm here on an unrelated call. I'm doing some legal business for the family that requires me to talk to Mister Parmenter."

"You a lawyer?"

"No, sir," Hoyt replied, whipping out his badge. "Private investigator."

"Wait outside," the cop told him. "You better come inside, Mister Parmenter, and see what the damage is."

Damage was an understatement. The place looked as if the ceiling had replaced the floor in a massive explosion. Everything smashed or broken. Even the sofa cushions and mattress in the bedroom gutted, stuffing lying all over.

"There's a lot of glass," one cop said, "so watch where you step."

"Any idea who might have done this?"

"No, officer, I don't."

"What's with all these steel cans on the floor?"

"He must have tossed my garbage around," Butchie said.

He heard Hoyt snickering behind him through the broken glass pane on the screen door. He stood on the steps close enough to hear everything.

"He wasn't too worried about anybody hearing him," the officer jotting down Butchie's personal information said. "Middle of the day and he's busting up the place. Was he looking for anything?"

"I don't own anything worth much," Butchie said. "A stereo system and a TV. That's it."

"He wasn't interested in those. He smashed them to smithereens. It looks personal to me, Mister Parmenter. Hey, I know you, I think. You're a member of Eastside Fratellanza. My name's Arlotti."

"Yeah, I haven't been there in a while," Butchie said.

"Funny," Arlotti said.

"What's funny?"

"He didn't smash your phone on the countertop," Arlotti said.

"He probably didn't know what it was," Butchie replied. City workers were required to have a landline.

"Come on, Arlotti," the other cop said, "if you two paisanos are done schmoozing." To Butchie, he said: "We'll send a Robbery detective over, but it might be a while."

As the officer pushed the door aside, Hoyt appeared behind it, a dangerous kid without a Halloween bag.

"Excuse us," Arlotti said to him in passing.

"Whoohie, he really fucked up your place, didn't he?"

"I don't recall inviting you in, Hoyt," Butchie said, still surveying the damage. Nothing was left unbroken or intact. Even Butchie's handball trophies were smashed. The big plasma TV he'd spent a fortune on was crazed like a broken mirror; he'd spent most of an afternoon mounting it on the wall, driving to DIY to purchase special shims he'd then had to cut on the circular saw at the garage, all because of the shoddy apartment construction.

"I look like a fucking vampire or something? You got to invite me in? You invited me in, asshole, when you stole that money from the Bello family."

"Get the fuck out of my house, you shitheel gumshoe."

Hoyt kicked him in the solar plexus before Butchie had taken a second step toward him.

Butchie dropped to the floor amid the debris and broken glass. His muscle spasms curled him into a ball involuntarily, as if to reduce the pain.

"Breathe," Hoyt said from above. "You'll be fine in a minute. Hurts like hell but it won't leave a bruise."

Hoyt, the evil magician who'd transformed him from man to curled-up baby on his floor, proved right. In a minute, he could draw air into his lungs without gasping. His breathing subsided to a hoarse wheeze and then to normal.

"A mass of nerves there," Hoyt said, smiling; "the word our hand-to-hand instructor called it was 'ganglia.'" Hoyt laughed at the memory. "'A ganglia of nerves,' he said. What a crazy prick. Face you could take a dump on, but he knew his combat shit. You'll fuck anybody up that way, he said, and you won't have to bruise your hands."

Butchie made it to his knees. The rise to a standing position seemed like climbing the north face of the Eiger just then so he stayed down, wobbling on his haunches.

"What's wrong, Parmenter? Your pussy hurt? Get up. If I

wanted to hurt you, your dumb ass would be hurt."

"What is it with you guys anyway?"

"What's with what guys?"

"You tough guys. Shake hands like girls, kick with your feet."

"Maybe someday when we're fuck buddies, I'll tell you all about my adventures in Iraq and Afghanistan. Wanna hear my war stories, Butchie?"

"I'd like you to leave, Hoyt. I asked you nicely and you kicked me in the stomach."

"No, I distinctly recall you were rude to me. Don't be rude to me. I'm your salvation, you dumb dick. You might not think it, but I can be your best friend. I can save you from more of this." He swept his hand around the room like a magician twirling a cape.

"How can you save me from this?"

"Give me the money, Butchie. Just fucking hand it over. Right now. And it ends here. The family won't prosecute. I'll see to it. I'll make sure Odraye Suggs goes away. He'll be locked up."

"I don't know anyone by that name," Butchie said.

Hoyt barked a laugh. "Of course, you don't. Here's another card in case you do remember his name."

Butchie swatted it out of Hoyt's hand before Hoyt could jam it into his shirt front pocket. Hoyt watched it flutter in the air like a baseball card kids used to flip on school playgrounds in an innocent time.

Hoyt's Cheshire cat smile popped into place as if cued. Butchie watched it disappear, mesmerized, when Hoyt seemed to tilt sideways and before Butchie could launch himself out of the way, a sweeping leg kick sent him flying headfirst over his upended sofa into the wall. His head left a cratered dent.

"I told you not to be rude to me, didn't I?"

Hoyt's voice seemed to float all around Butchie in stereo. Then it faded, and he felt the room's light mysteriously darken to a growing blackness while tiny glitters sparkled in the corners of his eyes, dozens of red and green fireflies, all trying to get inside his brain to wake him up.

The last thing he heard was the broken door being tossed aside and falling to the floor. Butchie figured going into the dream's blackness was, all in all, the best thing he could do at the moment, so he did.

CHAPTER 15

A bag of frozen peas on the back of his head helped. Odraye—who else?—had ripped the freezer door off as well as the main door in his search for the money. He'd rooted through the food to make sure Butchie hadn't stuck a couple hundred thousand behind the mayo and the pickle jars. The bags of frozen vegetables were no longer ice-cold but cold enough to slow down the growing bump on the back of his head.

Butchie paced in front of his window holding the bag of peas until he realized a small crowd of onlookers, his neighbors, were out there on the lawn looking in at him and the damage to his place. He wanted to go out to his Jeep to check the bags of money, make sure they were still there. He'd tossed them in back with his duffel bag and tennis racquets, baseball bats and gloves, a bachelor's junk trunk. They were too big to hide in the small compartment where the tire-changing equipment was stored. A random thief could slice through the plastic window with a box cutter, reach inside, and haul them off—take about half-a-minute, yet he didn't feel safe hiding them anywhere with all the eyes on him.

He drew the drapes across the window. "Note to self," he said, "don't piss off Dominic Hoyt."

What had Delores called him—cabrón?—that meant "bastard," he thought. Good word for that crooked-smiling prick. Why couldn't he be one of those harmless-looking, greasy types or the Hollywood leading-man type too afraid to fight because it might damage his looks? Butchie didn't need another psychopath in his life right then.

Butchie stopped at the Fratellanza Club. He wanted to ask Joe De Luca for some cop advice about the report he was told to fill out about the break-in. He wanted a cover story, something he could use to cover Hoyt's real visit and his connection to Odraye Suggs. But Joe had met a girl online at a dating site called Plenty of Fish, and they'd gone out to dinner at one of Brockton's Italian restaurants, had drinks at a bar six notches above Bittaker's.

Whatever switch got flipped in his head during his conversation with Suggs just got reinforced by Hoyt's visit. Butchie's mind might be stuck at a crazy angle, but he wasn't giving the money to either one of those sonsofbitches, not one miserable, outdated, raggedy-assed dollar bill.

He took chances, blew through caution lights and a couple red ones to get to Delores' place. His best hope was to tear off part of this coalition and so far Delores was the only one who talked to him and had nothing to gain by ruining him. He understood her motivation for going along with it: her kids. What, after all, were his? Theirs? Everybody's hands were dirty. If he could get her on his side, used whatever persuasion he had, he had half-a-chance to come out of this with his skin intact and maybe some of the loot. He'd work out later with his conscience how much. The main thing, the only thing right now, was to thwart the forces of darkness arrayed against him. Butchie's Catholic upbringing made it his way to see things in black and white, good and evil.

He saw her Toyota parked in a different slot this time, but she was home. Whether she had company was the big question.

Butchie took the Beretta out of the glove box and worked the slide, popping rounds, to get the feel of the gun. Then he reloaded, replaced the magazine, and tucked it behind his belt. He had Jelks's S & W in his belt. Armed fore and aft, he stayed put behind the wheel a moment longer, hands clenching the wheel, needing time to collect his thoughts and steady his breathing.

He did a fast scissor-walk across the street to her Toyota and then beelined for the stairwell. Taking the steps two and three at a time, he was outside her door in seconds.

The same quick three raps on the wood. He stood away from the peephole.

Nothing.

Same formula: three raps, one hand under his shirt for a fast draw.

Please God, don't let it snag on my BVDs if Odraye's waiting inside.

More nothing. Butchie gave it five long minutes, casting nervous glances behind him and jumping at the sound of traffic coming close.

He went back down the stairs and eased up to the double window for a peek inside. Quinnel told him he wasn't ready to rent this one out yet, but to come back when he was done. He had more work inside to do. Butchie saw sawhorses and planking with a jigsaw and some tools; canvas covered the floor. Cans of paint and brushes were lined against one wall.

Butchie sidled over to the Toyota. The hood was warm but whether from the sun or being driven recently, he couldn't tell. Messy, drink cups tossed into the passenger's wheel well. Empty water bottles, one plugged to the top with cigarette butts: Diz Jelks, the human chimney.

Butchie went to his Wrangler and opened the gate. He rooted among the camouflaged junk he'd scattered around with the money bags and found a tire lever.

He raced back up to the top and slammed the beveled edge into the top corner, something he'd done on the job dozens of times in many abandoned and decayed houses. He pried the door off its hinge and then did the same with the bottom. Voilà, a revolving door. Her chain lock kept it from falling but he was inside, gun out in a two-handed grip.

Unlike the car, the interior was neat except for some dirty dishes in the sink. Nobody home.

He kept close to the walls as he headed toward her bedroom. The bathroom door first. Nothing.

The bedroom door was cracked. Carpeting made it easy to walk in silence; still, his heart pounded the closer he got to it.

She could be out for a walk, a short trip to the Save-A-Lot around the corner on Ashland.

But she wasn't out for a walk. She was on the bed, nude, on her stomach. The dark furrow of her sex visible between her parted legs. Butchie lowered the gun.

He wanted to feel for a pulse but his limbic brain was screaming for him to haul anchor and get out of there fast before he left more DNA for the forensics team to find.

Butchie felt he owed her that much before he bolted. He walked around the bed to avoid touching her. The feet sticking out from the other side were men's shoes; the trouble was, they weren't flat on the carpet but perpendicular to the ceiling and the reason for that was because there was a body still inside them. The body belonged to Maurice Jelks. He was fully clothed, dapper even, sandwiched into the narrow space next to the bed. The bullet hole under his chin clashed with the devil-may-care expression on his face that the bandage across his nose couldn't disguise. Maybe the expanding gases from the muzzle fire released inside his head accounted for it, Butchie thought, but it sickened him nonetheless. A stippling of soot ringed the hole's circumference. The gun had been placed on the skin when fired; a ragout of brains and blood formed dark brown rosettes like leopard spots on the wall beside his head.

Butchie didn't think there was any point to lingering in the room, but he never liked half gestures. He reached out to touch Delores' neck. Cold skin, no pulse. He shifted her head slightly with his fingertips and saw the damage; she'd been shot through the left eyeball. When he saw the flies tucked into the hole laying eggs, he snapped upright like a marionette.

Slowly, he retraced his steps backwards out of the room. At the bathroom door, he felt the gush in his esophagus and there was nothing for it but to get his head inside the toilet bowl as fast as possible. He vomited until his stomach protested with knife pains. Butchie prayed the toilet's water pump didn't take a long time to refill. He flushed three times, wiped down the rim of the bowl and the base of the toilet in case he'd spewed up something they could bag.

He figured the killer wasn't setting a trap by watching him walk into the apartment. The cops would have arrived by now. He set about wiping down everything he might have touched. He even took her vacuum cleaner out and ran it backwards from her bedroom to the door and then he removed the bag.

Quinnel's mother's house was isolated in its own section of the street. Both houses on either side had been boarded up by the city long ago. Butchie had inspected the one on the opposite side of the street years before it became a needle academy for neighborhood junkies. The owner, a Florida retiree, refused to let go of the property until the city condemned it as an eyesore and nuisance. Somebody wasn't bothered by the kids who played on the tire swing attached to the limb of the willow a hundred feet away or the fact that Quinnel Jones worked sporadic hours on the house during his free time from his regular job.

Butchie hesitated opposite the downstairs door. He slapped the lever against his fist and figured he had to know. This door wasn't visible to any other house, so he took his time breaking it free from the hinges. He used his elbow to flick on the lights.

He moved around slowly. Checking under a bump in the canvas cloth on the floor. He checked the two back rooms. Quinnel was in the bathroom at the end of the corridor. He was hanging from the shower. His pants were undone and his semi-erect member had drooled jizz. Butchie noted the pool that had spilled onto Quinnel's feet and pasted his toes.

That was enough, too much. He had to get out of there even if his stomach had emptied upstairs. This was a horror show beyond anything he had ever expected to see or to deal with in his lifetime.

Outside, on shaky legs, he zigzagged to the Jeep and hoisted himself up, panting, sick at heart at the monsters unleashed in his life. The murder-suicide upstairs was faked. Quinnel was no sexual asphyxiation. The killer was tying off another loose end. He hoped the Brockton M.E. was good enough to find the clues on Quinnel's remains.

Butchie recalled his last conversation with Jones. The streets had raised him and done the job badly as with so many young men of his generation. But he'd found a way out after his last bid for a botched snatch-and-grab job of an ATM machine. Beneath the gang tattoos and the prison patter of his conversation, Butchie sensed decency. The recollection made him wince. What had he done to throw his birthright away, his integrity, like brother Esau his for a mess of porridge?

Butchie wasn't sure he could find the answer. Before he drove out of the lot, he looked backward once and said, "I'm sorry." None of the ghosts he was accumulating answered back.

CHAPTER 16

Butchie didn't think Odraye was crazy enough to attack him in the same place twice, but with an active volcano, who can say how long the plug stayed in?

One of his first thoughts when counting the money in his garage was to get fake papers and blow town. Take it to some bank out of state, open an account, lay out a story that wasn't too whackjob to the cashier or bank manager, and deposit the money. Wait a week, get a cashier's check and point his Wrangler toward Key West. Butchie knew some shady people in Brockton—who didn't? But he knew none who could be classed as "archcriminal." Neecie, however, had a distant cousin from Boston who sometimes showed up at family christenings and weddings. Butchie had met him at once and he remembered Neecie whispering in his ear while they danced to some wedding tune about her cousin Paulie Donato. Paulie was the family black sheep.

"Neecie, it's me."

"Oh Jesus."

"No, just one of his lost sheep," Butchie replied.

"Butchie, you ain't even half-funny. What do you want?"

"I need Paul Donato's number."

"Why?"

"I might be out of a job soon. Your cousin works for Amtrak in Boston. You gotta know somebody on the railroad to get a job there."

Silence, Neecie thinking it over.

"I don't know."

"C'mon, babe, for auld lang syne."

"Honest to God, Butchie, you never quit, do you?"

"I swear it, Neecie. You know Asaro's had it in for me for years. Now he's got a reason to fire me. I just had a disciplinary hearing. It didn't go so good."

"You wonder why?"

Butchie figured the Catholic Church had made a big mistake letting priests and bishops do the interrogating during the Spanish Inquisition; it would have been smarter to let the women do it and they could save themselves the trouble of torturing the heretics.

"No, I don't, Neecie. But that won't help me get a new job, will it?"

Butchie sensed her relenting in the pause. He and she were on the same wavelength even when they were apart. One reason for holding on to all the money was the slender hope she'd come back to him, and only money makes it possible. A quarter-million does it, half of that gives you a head start on the wolf pack.

She gave him the numbers.

"Thanks, Neecie, look, I'm—"

Click, gone. No goodbye even.

Paul Donato agreed to meet him at Bittaker's later in the day. Butchie used his credit card for a room in a budget motel off Christy Drive. It was close to the highway in case he needed a fast exit away from town. All cities had lockdown plans since 9/11. Brockton could be slammed shut with roadblocks in twenty minutes. "Now I'm thinking like a criminal," he muttered.

He drove home to get some clothes and supplies. He didn't know when it would be safe to return, but he didn't plan on sleeping there with Odraye loose. He didn't bother sneaking through a window or going around where he'd be obscured somewhat by the red maple out back. A big red-lettered aluminum Neighborhood Watch Sign posted out front on the curb—WE REPORT ALL SUSPICIOUS ACTIVITY IN THIS NEIGHBORHOOD. He charged right through the front door at high noon. Odraye showed he could wipe his ass with that bench warrant.

Butchie picked up toiletries off the floor and stuffed them into his duffel bag. Odraye had ransacked the bathroom for good measure, even jamming the shower curtain into the toilet. He must have been in a terrible rage when Jelks came back with a broken nose and no Butchie in tow.

On his way out, Butchie propped the door against the frame as best he could.

"Going somewhere?"

Butchie didn't need to turn around: Dominic Hoyt.

"Maybe you noticed my place is a little messy, Dom," he said. "Thought I'd crash on a friend's sofa tonight."

"That sounds like a good idea. Say, you wouldn't be driving around with that money, would you, Butchie?"

"You want to check it, see for yourself?"

"No, I believe you. Even you can't be that dumb."

"You're assuming I have it, Hoyt. That's a wrong assumption. I don't have the money. This place, what happened here, has nothing to do with the money. I got a problem with a guy at work. I been dating his ex and he thinks she should be in a nunnery pining for him. Now why don't you fuck off and leave me alone?"

"Dating his ex, huh? The jealous ex, that what you're saying did this? Sounds like some movie melodrama going on there, Butchie."

"That's what it is, Dom. You got it in one."

"You like movies, Butchie?"

"I love them. I grew up watching Dario Argento films. That's how I got my philosophy of life."

"I would have guessed you liked westerns. I hate movies, myself. But you think it's all gonna play out like High Noon. The good guy rides off into the sunset with the prize."

Hoyt was creeping him out. Butchie rented High Noon so many times his father hid the video on him under the couch.

"I never saw it," Butchie lied.

"Western. Gary Cooper, nineteen-fifty-two," Hoyt replied.

"Saw it on the Turner Channel at the motel the other night. This town marshal in some pisshole on the prairie, he's blowing town on a buckboard with his new bride, some young blonde gash—a school marm—before the three bad guys come in on the noon train to kill him."

"Never saw it," Butchie repeated. "Tell me, does he make it—I mean, with the blonde gash as you so eloquently put it?"

"Absolutely he makes it. It's Hollywood. He kills all the bad guys and gets the girl. She's the only prize, the blonde, if she was blonde. Even then, they made them dye. No IRAs or retirement pensions, no big pile of cash to spend in the golden years. Just her blonde pussy."

"I'll be sure to add that one to my Netflix watch list," Butchie said. "You mind letting me pass?"

Hoyt stayed put at the bottom of the steps. Butchie thought about his chances of walking by but the memory of those sweeping leg kicks kept him rooted to the top of the steps as if somebody had driven ten-penny nails through his shoes.

Hoyt grimaced. His cat-smile didn't show up. "I believe you—up to a point," he said. "I think whoever trashed your place thinks you have it. Makes sense for me to keep an eye on you. See if you start digging up any coffee cans full of money buried in a field nearby. I know you didn't rent space in a storage facility. I've been showing your photo around."

"Maybe you should follow me to my local bank, Hoyt. Could be it's in a safe-deposit box."

"Nope, not you, Butchie. That's not you."

"You watch too many movies, Dom."

"I don't watch many movies, Butchie. You know why?"

"No time? Too busy kicking the daylights out of people?"

"That never takes much time. See, Butchie, if you're in a real fight, you don't waste time like in movies. Guys throwing punches guaranteed to break metacarpal bones and then standing there looking to see what they did. You put your man down however you have to and you keep him down. First rule of fighting, don't let yourself be hurt."

"I see. Action films are your thing."

"No," Hoyt said, seeming to pause to think about it.

Butchie knew the longer he stood there, the longer Hoyt could keep him treed like a possum. Only problem, a big one, he wasn't out of reach of Hoyt's fists or feet.

"They don't match up to reality," Hoyt continued, as if they were a couple cinema buffs enjoying a chat on a midsummer day in Brockton like any two ordinary human beings.

"Not the explosions and car wrecks and guys getting shot-to-shit-and-back, all that massive firepower like walking up to some towelhead or greaser and twisting the AR out of his hands while he's spraying bullets. You remember what I said about the solar plexus?"

"Come to think of it, I do, yes," Butchie said.

"You can't get shot in the shoulder and keep throwing punches. Shoulder's got the same mass of major blood vessels and zillions of nerve endings. Nine times of ten, that's where the hero gets shot, right? Yet he's still fighting, shooting the bad guys. That's just not how it is. Look here."

Hoyt pulled his right sleeve up his shoulder and turned his body to give Butchie a look. A starburst of puckered skin and long white scar lines from surgery like the tails of cilia under a microscope.

"What's your point, hero? I'm busy. I've got things to do."

"It's people they get wrong every time," Hoyt said. "People just don't act like Hollywood thinks they do. I've seen tough guys. Most of them are normal looking—but that's where it stops. I know what they are and I know what they can do to human beings."

"One more feather in your cap, huh? Now you're a big-shot film critic. I'm amazed, Dom, I really am."

"I'm a lot of things, Butchie. A true Renaissance man, some might say. Another thing about me is I don't appreciate sarcasm. Don't make me show you some of my less obvious skills, little tricks I picked up around the Helmand Province. Some of them you don't ever want to find out about. Or there could be a great reckoning in a small room. Take care now. See you around."

"Go to hell."

Hoyt walked off whistling a familiar tune.

For a guy who says he doesn't like movies, Butchie thought, he sure as shit sounds like a Hollywood tough guy. 'Great reckoning'. . . it sounded like some literary shit the nuns used to din in their students' ears back in grade school. Hoyt and those hatchet-faced nuns in one image: that was the scary part, too.

Butchie didn't like the idea of having Dominic Hoyt on his tail all the way to the motel, so he headed for Bittaker's after cashing a credit-card check at the bank. He'd done that before when his gambling fever got too high and he ran short after a losing streak.

Thinking of Hoyt whistling the High Noon theme sent a ripple of fear up his back. It didn't seem like a coincidence. Nothing about Hoyt was spontaneous. Butchie wondered if he could have spotted the DVD jacket of High Noon among the debris in his house and was making a point, all that stuff about tough guys and Hollywood creampuffs acting like tough guys.

It's like he's seeing into me, Butchie thought, gauging my character from the films I watch. Butchie felt a queasy spasm in his stomach. Hoyt was a hyena looking around for a limp. Butchie's boyhood addiction to cowboy films revealed him, especially after he started having trouble with the Irish and the blacks in their new house after his father lost his job. Butchie wanted to believe in something in the here and now, not all that sugar-coated, fairy-tale crap the nuns handed out about guardian angels and saints watching out for us. Nobody's watching out. He was fourteen when he came to the realization he was on his own.

Butchie figured he'd nurse a beer or two and wait for Donato to show. Wash the taste of Hoyt out of his system.

Three beers and a couple shots later, Donato showed and took the stool beside him.

"Butchie, what's shakin'? You still engaged to my cousin?"

"Denise dumped me months ago, Paulie."

"Too bad. She's a nice girl. You probably did something to deserve it."

Butchie held up two fingers and pointed at his empty glass. Bobby looked his way and gave him the finger and resumed his conversation with the female sitting opposite him.

"That Bobby?"

"Yeah," Butchie said. "He's still here. Where you been, you didn't know that?"

"Traveling," Paulie said.

"Traveling for work? I thought you quit the railroad," Butchie said.

It was common knowledge Donato was fired for cause. His pickup truck was found wedged into a ditch when he tried to make a three-corner turn to get away with the swag he'd stolen from a boxcar parked on a siding in the Boston railyards. Under the tarp, railroad security found boxes of Nintendo Wiis, PlayStation 4s, and fifty cases of premium microbrewery beer.

Butchie was relieved Bobby Steele brought over fresh drinks for him and a draft beer for Paul without stopping to chat. He immediately went back to his girl at the other end of the bar.

"Damn, Bobby," Paul said watching the bartender retreat, "what happened to bros before hoes?"

"I need some papers," Butchie said.

"What kind of papers?"

"The kind that'll stand up to a credit-card check. Social security, credit card—"

"Hold it there, Butchie, you're talking about four, maybe five thousand right there, and I ain't your guy."

"You must know somebody in Boston who can do them. Cash up front," Butchie said, "no problem."

"What the fuck, man, did you hit the lottery while I was out of town?"

"No, it's an inheritance."

"An inheritance . . . OK, I'll buy that," Donato said. "I'll make some calls. Give me your digits."

Butchie handed over his cell phone and watched Paulie punch in the numbers.

"How soon?"

"Shit, I don't know. That ain't my gig, yo."

"Neecie thinks you're still with the railroad."

"I am," he said. "I'm a cargo pilferage specialist."

"You're still stealing from the railroad," Butchie replied.

"Hell's-bells, man, anybody with a crowbar, bolt cutters, and a little testosterone can steal from the railroad."

"It can't be that easy or half the bozos in town would be doing it," Butchie laughed.

"They are, man. The competition's keen, I'm telling you! You see a train go by, a mile long, how many ain't got gang graffiti on 'em? Don't tell me about railroad anti-theft security when any fifteen-year-old idiot with a can of Silver Brite can get that close to your copper, computer components, and pharmaceuticals."

"How much of that can you fence?"

"The big stuff, you mean?"

"No, I mean generic dog food and cases of ketchup," Butchie said.

"Well, truth be told, I wind up with more of that shit than I do the high-value goods, but yeah, I get a decent dollar on the exchange. Most, not all. Butchie, before you ask, I ain't lookin' for no partners."

"I wasn't asking to join you in a jail cell someday, Paulie."

"It's risky, I'll admit. But, man, a train on a siding with just a two-man crew sitting idle in a locomotive a half-mile ahead in the dark—man, that freight is ripe for pickings."

"I just need the papers. I'm kinda in a rush here," Butchie said.

Paul sucked down the last of his beer. "I'll be in touch, kiddo. Stay loose."

"Where you staying?" Butchie asked.

"Here and there," Donato said.

Christ, another man of mystery. . .

Butchie thought about trains. He loved listening to train whistles as a teenager—still did, especially at night. That mournful sound thrilled something in him. He didn't know what it was because everything was simpler back then. Simple as those old-time, black-and-white cowboy films, which brought Dominic Hoyt back into his mind, front and center. Butchie suddenly didn't like the taste of his whiskey. He put a ten on the bar for Bobby and got off the stool.

The sun smacked him in the face and the muggy air carried a scent of frying grease. Something else, too, less sharp, the pungent smell of swamp rot. Butchie faced east. If he could run fast enough, plow through buildings like Superman, he could hit Plymouth Bay in no time and clean himself of the filth, the lies, the grit, and all the anxiety of these last few days.

Opening the Jeep's door, he stopped suddenly and noticed somebody had keyed the side of his Jeep from fender to fender. He flashed back to Hoyt walking off from his apartment, whistling something.

That sonofabitch lied about that, too. He does like movies. The recollection of Hoyt's nonchalant exit from the steps of his apartment sent a shiver up his spine. The guy was a pretentious thug, a narcissistic brute. Yet he had managed with the simple gesture of whistling a tune to twist Tex Ritter's romantic lyrics into a menacing ballad.

"Don't Forsake Me, Oh My Darling. . ."

'She's the only prize'. . .

God damn, he's threatening me with Neecie—

CHAPTER 17

"What are you talking about? You sound like a crazy man."

"Neecie, just listen to me for once, all right? Call Anthony. I'll call Anthony. But tell him he needs to keep an eye on you. There's this guy—"

"What guy? Are you out of your mind? What kind of trouble are you into now, Butchie, because I swear if you get my family mixed up in anything, I'll call the cops on you myself."

"Whoooah, Jesus fuck shit, motherfucker. . ."

"What? What? Butchie, what?"

"Nothing, sorry, Neecie. This asshole swerved right into me—nearly clipped me. I'm just crossing Centre on Montebello now. I'll be there in ten minutes."

"No, you won't," Neecie said. "You show up here, my father said he'll kick your ass. Antony's been buggin' me every day. He thinks I'm seeing you again."

"I can't explain it," Butchie said. "It's complicated."

"Oh, Christ, complicated. Are you drunk? You sound drunk. You better not be smoking weed again."

"Neecie, just wait for me and don't go outside, you hear me? Don't leave the house until we talk."

Butchie cut her off before she could say anything else. All his fears of Odraye had magically transferred themselves into a bundle and landed on his shoulders; it was Hoyt, the bastard, who could have followed him to Quinnel's and killed all three. He's no white knight working for the Bello family. He's still a mercenary and Brockton is just an extension of Afghanistan with more traffic signs. You don't leave that behind. Butchie couldn't be sure if his paranoia was getting to him or whether Hoyt's harping on that film meant anything.

Butchie was sure of one thing: he was alive because he had the money. But everybody else was fair game. He'd tossed a rock into a pond and he couldn't stop the ripples. They just kept going and going.

He saw her sitting on her porch reading the paper. No Anthony, no Mr. DiGiacomo with a shotgun. So far, so good.

"Neecie, thank God," Butchie said, taking the steps two at a time.

She stood up abruptly. He recognized the pinched nostrils, the tight pursed lips, Cupid Bow lips that matched her oval face and long chestnut hair.

He lifted his hands to take her in his arms. She sidestepped him and hit him across the face with the paper.

Butchie stood there, stunned, touching his lips and seeing blood come away. She'd rolled it up and belted him good with it.

He picked it up in front of the swing where it lay. He and Neecie had spent long hours necking and petting right here after the family had gone to bed.

He turned it over. The headline was a second swat across the face:

Triple Murder Shocks Neighbors

Worse always comes to worse, doesn't it, Pop?

Neecie was at least calm enough to walk him to the door. He'd spent two long hours groveling over his mistakes and recent experiences. She listened patiently and asked a few questions. Butchie was grateful she kept the recriminations for his boneheadedness to a minimum. He was lucky both her parents were visiting relatives in Boston for a couple days. The thought of trying to explain everything that went on from the Bello store to Hoyt's last visit was unthinkable.

"You're lucky my dad isn't here, you know that?"

"Christ, Neecie, I'd just as soon blow my own head off before trying to explain this clusterfuck to him."

"You have to give that money back."

She'd said that so many times in the last hour it was imprinted on his neocortex, but he didn't try to refute it or agree to it.

"You're nodding your head again," she said. "Does that mean yes or no?"

"It might not be that simple. Look, all that matters right now is that you pack up some things and we drive to your sister's place. You can't stay here. I can't bear the thought of anything happening to you. This guy Hoyt, he's dangerous."

"You're going to wind up in the morgue," she said.

Butchie convinced her finally when he showed her the eggplant-shaped bruise on his leg where Hoyt had kicked him and the knot on his head.

He followed her to the sister's house in Framingham studying every vehicle behind them until it turned off. Neecie had packed a single overnight bag. Standing in the driveway near the cars, she told him not to come in. Butchie looked toward the house and saw her two nieces and two nephews peeking at them through the picture window and waving frenetically. Butchie realized he had alienated her entire family when their engagement ended, no matter that she had given him the walking papers.

Watching her go inside, he backed out of the driveway and almost hit a car passing by. The Doppler effect of the car horn wailing all the way down the street sent shock waves through his brittle system; he knew he wasn't eating right, drinking way too much, and not getting enough good sleep.

The two bags of old money lay in the back obscured by an old duvet and his other props.

It's just a bunch of old paper, Butchie told himself as he drove back to Brockton. That's all it is—old paper with a rough feel to it. Look at all the shit coming down on me because of it. Jesus Christ, it's like one of those shitty folk songs from the sixties without the fifty dead sailors at the bottom of the sea or the silver stallion running in the moonlight with a dagger in its eye.

That depends, doesn't it, Butchie, the little voice in his head replied.

Depends, how? Butchie said, playing along with his alter ego in the Jeep.

Depends on how it ends, motherfucker.

Damn, if the voice didn't suddenly sound like Hoyt's.

As if the man's very image, dwarf-sized—a homunculus Hoyt—had been summoned from the depths and transplanted through spacetime to occupy the seat beside him, the way those old nuns used to talk about the gargoyles on cathedral roofs, tiny Hoyt looked at Butchie from the passenger seat and smiled that Cheshire smile at him.

"We'll just see about that," Butchie said to the phantom—and whipped the Jeep at the last second before colliding with the SUV in front of him. Butchie saw the anxious mother's face in the window as he careened past, fighting the wheel for control. She had a car full of kids.

Butchie wondered if it was finally time to pray again. The spit dried in his mouth when he attempted to say The Lord's Prayer. He tried it in Latin, dredging up ancient memories of serving mass for Fr. Montesanti until his drinking got too bad and they whisked him off to the old home for priests, wherever that was. "Pater noster, qui es in cælsis. . ." but he couldn't remember the rest. He tried some random words that began the same way: Dear Father in Heaven, Holy Lord, Heavenly Father, but he might as well have begun with the Qur'an: "In the name of Allah, the Most Beneficent, the Most Merciful. . ." Zero, nada, zilch. He was like most of his friends who were lapsed Catholics. They believed in death-bed confessions after an adulthood of ignoring the faith of their youth. He took it as nature that blunted self-awareness as he aged rather than his own decisions. Like most people who believe we all die someday, Butchie hoped there'd be one exception. Facing the disaster of his life wasn't easy under the best of circumstances and these were far from it.

Odraye or Hoyt? The seething anger behind the murders implied Suggs. The staging suggested Hoyt. Butchie wondered: Did it matter?

He called Neecie again but got her voicemail. Last time he called, she said to stop checking up on her, she was fine. Butchie knew how fast "fine" could change.

CHAPTER 18

The drive back to his motel took twice the time; he circled it like a cur sniffing garbage, cut down some side streets and swung over to the curb several times to see if he was being followed. He'd stopped for cigarettes and beer at a convenience store two blocks from Christy. Last year, he'd described his quitting smoking to Bobby as being stuffed into a shit-chute with no way out. They said the psychology of quitting was harder than the physical. "That's bullshit," he told Bobby. "I wanted to smoke every other second for two weeks because my lungs were screaming for it." Now he was back in the barrel.

He sat on the bed with his knees curled and listened to traffic noises outside. The air-conditioner thrummed and the pipes knocked but not so loud he'd be unable to sleep. The room smelled like chicken noodle soup, a smell he always associated with body odor.

Butchie got up to sit on the toilet and smoke a cigarette before he downed another beer. The alcohol sloshed on his empty stomach, which helped. One more Heineken and he'd sleep a couple, three hours—a gun under each pillow. He'd think of his next move when he woke, but right now, the drowsiness and the heat of the day blistering the parking lot and raising smells of asphalt cooking were too powerful to overcome. He'd done the right thing calling Paul Donato to get him papers; plenty of banks would accept the money and not ask too many questions. He'd square things with Neecie. Have her fly out to meet him and they'd take a long drive down Highway 1 to the Keys. Maybe he'd pick out a small bungalow or a nice doublewide in one of the smaller Keys away from the cotton-haired, bandy-legged tourists in their loud colors and parrot shirts, not to mention the New England snowbirds he didn't want to see or hear ever again. They could start over. Have a family. . . Butchie snapped to from his daydream, his heart doing a bongo solo in his chest.

This shit can't end well, he thought. I'll be sticking my head up checking out who's coming up on me all the rest of my life like some prairie gopher looking out for coyotes.

He hopped off and took the Pico and the two green Heinekens and wrapped them in a towel. He held them upside down over the sink and tapped the bottoms until they broke. He kept hitting the glass through the towel until he had several large pieces. He dumped the splinters in the waste basket and threw the towel away. He placed the pieces behind the door where anybody creeping in would be likely to step first.

He replaced the Beretta under the second pillow and felt for the bigger gun under his own pillow, practicing pulling it out several times, inserting a memory muscle if he had to draw it in a big hurry.

He closed his eyes; the drowsy feeling wasn't there now. Instead, his eyes had a will of their own and demanded to be opened wide fixated on the rectangle of brown door for approaching danger.

He tried to will himself to sleep. Who was that guy in Greek myth who was dying of thirst and starving for food? Fr. Montesanti used him for a moral lesson more than once but he always tuned the old priest out when he started droning at the lectern. Butchie had other things to think about then, mainly girls and sports. The gods wanted to punish the guy for all eternity that way because of what he'd done. What the hell had he done to deserve that? Butchie couldn't remember. He imagined the boughs of fruit withdrawing from his reach like the Rock's right arm stuck in midair. Butchie saw himself in the waist-deep water he'd never be able to slake his thirst with. Two shapes loomed into view from opposite banks: Hoyt with his crooked smile on one side of him and Suggs on the other. In the crazy logic of dreams, the water became a murky river; he was trying to cross it midstream. A pair of eyeballs broke the surface and tiny waves broke at snouts and thrashing tails: crocodiles. Butchie had to move fast. . . His heart was banging in his chest as he lunged through the water making no progress while those massive reptiles bore down on him. . .

Thud, thud, thud.

He shot upright in bed, fumbling with his groping fingers beneath the pillow for the gun butt, unable to find it. His throat released a sob, stark terror climbing up his spine and warbling in his brain like a bandsaw, expecting any second the door to come flying off its hinges and—

"Parmenter, Butchie Parmenter! Open up, please! This is Detective Forshey. I want a word with you."

"Give us some credit, huh?"

Butchie's sleep-deprived body was in full revolt stuck in that tiny interrogation room with the temperature set to "Morgue." He'd been kept waiting twenty minutes as it was. One part of him was grateful it wasn't SWAT busting down the door.

"I wasn't hiding, you know," he said. "My place is a dump thanks to—my girl's ex. I signed in with my own name."

Forshey nodded. "Sure, Butchie, I know that."

The cop all but made the universal sign for masturbation to what Butchie was telling him, so he figured he'd better shut up. A little indignation at being rousted from his new digs was in order, however; the cop would expect that much.

"Can I get you get a blanket?" Forshey asked, setting a couple Styrofoam cups of coffee down on the table dividing them. "You look cold."

Butchie could not help the shivers. They came and went of their own accord.

"I appreciate you're coming down here," the cop said.

"Is that a joke?"

"No, I really mean it," Forshey responded.

"Ask your questions or read me that Miranda thing," he said.

"Easy there," Forshey laughed. "No one's arresting you or accusing you of anything. I mean it. I need help with the investigation. Half the Brockton cops are working this case now. You see all those Boston reporters outside?"

"No, I didn't," Butchie said.

The reason was Forshey had the uniform cops accompanying him drive around to the rear.

"I could have made you famous," Forshey added. "I didn't make you do the perp walk in front of the cameras."

"I'm supposed to be grateful? Come on, Forshey, quit dancing around here."

"OK, I need to know where you were and who you were with, say, in the last thirty-six hours. Here's paper." He shoved a tablet across the table. "Write it down. Don't leave out anything. I'll give you some time alone."

Butchie knew that was a crock of shit. He was on camera and he could only guess at the number of detectives crowded around the monitor watching his every move. He wrote, paused, looked up every few minutes, as if trying to recall some detail, but his brain was pinwheeling with things to say, not say, and not to even hint at. He'd learned from B.S.'ing Neecie years ago that a lie is difficult to maintain, and you wind up supporting it with more lies until it gets to be too much to remember.

Forty minutes passed. Butchie printed his name and signed it at the bottom and dated it.

Another half-hour passed before Forshey came back into the room.

"Hey, you didn't touch your coffee."

Butchie shrugged. He never gave it a second thought since the cop had placed it there. It had turned brackish on the surface, a gray scum with white globs of creamer bobbing on the surface. Butchie thought of Jelks on the floor where the blood and sere of his wound had separated. The dusting of soot around the hole. . .

"I don't blame you," Forshey said, although he'd brought in a fresh cup with him. "Crimes only get solved with coffee."

"Just like TV, huh?"

"Exactly like TV," Forshey replied. He reached for the tablet and riffed the pages, skimming what Butchie had written. At the last page, he looked up. "Tommaso? That really your name?"

"My mother had a brother who died of the croup as a baby," Butchie said. "Can we just get on with it, Forshey, because I am walking out in ten seconds if I don't get a straight answer why you brought me here."

"I would have thought that obvious, Parmenter. A woman says you raped her. Then she gets herself murdered in a not-too-pretty way in her own apartment along with a boyfriend and her landlord below. It'd be pretty obvious to most people why you're here."

"Why don't you read what I wrote down and you'll find out," he said.

"Oh, don't you worry about that. I've got three detectives right now running down the names of everybody you mentioned, including Trooper DeLuca, who's off shift and driving down here as we speak."

Butchie made a big deal of his short time at the Fratellanza Club after Hoyt's visit, even though he'd barely spoken to him for five minutes that time. He had to cover some big gaps in his timeline. He knew Paulie Donato would cover the disparity in time in the notebook without mentioning why Butchie called him.

"Look, I called her, as I said. I asked her to drop the charges."

"And she did, just like that. Why, Butchie? Why would she do that for you because you asked her pretty-please."

"She thought I'd be willing to—to give her money to do it," he said. "There was no merit to that charge in the first place."

Libeling the dead now, what a prick loser I am. . .

"OK, we're looking into that. Your boss Daniel Asaro

thinks there was enough merit to convene a disciplinary hearing."

"That never came up," Butchie said.

"Trouble seems to follow you lately," Forshey said.

"I don't know what you mean."

"Your place. Three people murdered. One you were accused of raping. Quinnel Jones, you gave his place a pass, right?"

"Yes."

"How much did he kick back to you for that deal? Never mind, I don't give a flying fuck about your chickenshit graft, Parmenter. I got bodies on the floor and you seem to be connected in some way to most of them."

"I explained all that—"

"Be quiet," Forshey said. He started ticking off items on his fingers.

"Four people die violently. One, your place gets smashed up by 'a jealous ex' after one date with a girl, a girl you never call back and who never calls you again. Yeah, we spoke to her. Two, you immediately go into hiding in some Crazy 8 motel. Three, Odraye Suggs. You say you only met him one time at the Bello store in Leotis Marsten's company. Marsten gets discovered dead upstairs covered in maggots with a hole in his skull you can put your fist through. You and this Suggs—with a record for selling drugs and thumping women around— just happen to be the last people to see Marsten alive. Want me to keep going?"

Butchie shrugged again. "You should be talking to this Suggs guy, not me."

"We'll find him, don't worry. We think he skipped once word got out. We know where he goes in Boston, the old Combat Zone, Chinatown, so we'll be talking to him soon. There's more."

"More what?"

Here it comes, Butchie thought.

"Rumors all over this town the Bello money was stolen by you and Suggs. Leotis Marsten witnessed you finding the cash and you refused to share it with him or else you three were in on it and there was a falling out of thieves and you two killed him."

"That's a lot to prove," Butchie said.

"Butchie, this is not my first rodeo. If there's anything you want to say, now is the time. I'm here to listen to your side of the story."

"I think every time a cop says that to someone in a room like this, the next thing the suspect hears is the cell closing behind him. I'm out of here, Detective. You want me to come down here again, you'll have to arrest me."

"You're making a mistake, Parmenter."

"I made a mistake coming here in the first place."

He half-expected a dozen beefy cops to burst out of the room next door and throw him to the floor and cuff him up. It didn't happen. He felt the nape of his neck tingle with suspense until he was all the way out of the building standing on the steps blinking into the sunlight. After the fierce cold of the interrogation room, the warmth enveloped him; he began to sweat heavily. By the time he made it to his Jeep, he was drenched in perspiration. Every pore in his body opened the floodgates.

Butchie started the Jeep and adjusted the rearview mirror to check the clutter of the storage area behind the gate. It looked undisturbed. He shook his head. He was driving around with a quarter-million dollars, followed by people who threatened him with guns, prison, and various sorts of mayhem. He was tired of being interrogated, punched and kicked, and all any one of these morons had to do was slit that plexiglass window back there and pull out the bags.

If that happens, Butchie thought, none of that will go away—and I still won't be able to get some sleep.

CHAPTER 19

"Did you find the dog?"

"What dog?"

"The one that took a dump in your mouth while you was sleeping."

"Fuck you, Paulie."

"Have a mint," Donato said. "Do something about that breath, man."

"My stomach's been off lately," Butchie said. "I thought you were gonna call me?"

The parking lot of the Fratellanza was half-full for this time of day. Usually just the "old dagos" showed up before five, the bocce players and the retirees.

"Let's get a drink," Butchie said. "It'll kill my germs."

"I can't come in. I'm seeing Lou Domenico downtown about a big construction deal we got going. A sweet Section Eight contract for prefabbing tract houses for the retards. But I got that business on track you wanted to take care of. My guy in Boston wants seven-five up front."

"Fuck, Paul, I'm not escaping to Argentina in a cloud of smoke. I just need a driver's license and a credit card."

"The price is firm. Take it or leave it."

"I'm leaving it," Butchie said.

"Your call. I gotta run. Good luck with—whatever."

Sweetheart deals, shortcuts, ripoffs, kickbacks. It's all this Sopranos-Godfather wet-your-beak bullshit, Butchie thought. It's infectious like a disease. It got me, too.

Butchie doubted there was ever a guy in Boston. Paulie was thinking of slicing off a share before they carved him up.

Butchie learned how fast rumor traveled when he went inside. He planned on killing a couple hours in the club. Leave his Jeep where anybody driving by could see it. He wanted to see who had eyes on him. He waved at some guys he knew at the bar and a few more at some tables. Mike Palumbo, he used to work with; Jerry Peet, he went to school with; Nicky Arcaro, he double-dated Penny and Pam, the Anderson twins in high school. Nobody came over. Nobody bought him a drink or stopped to chat. He sat alone at the stool and felt eyes boring through his back. 'Rumors,' Forshey had said when he had him in the box. They all know.

Butchie had never felt so alone in a crowd as he did that moment. He would never be able to rub the shit off his shoes.

He left his beer unfinished and drove to the nearest public library. Until he'd spoken to Paul in the parking lot, he thought it was possible to keep the money and his old life too. He now knew that was impossible. He was marked like Cain. He couldn't spend the rest of his life explaining to people that he didn't kill anybody. Yeah, I stole the money. So what? It was rotting behind an old refrigerator. Nobody walks by and leaves that kind of cash behind. Neecie's words rang in his ear: "The money's got blood all over it. You can't keep it."

"No, I can't keep it," Butchie admitted to her. But he couldn't give it back, either.

She'd hung up.

He used the library's computers, filched some discarded Xerox paper from a wastebasket, and asked the librarian for a pencil. She gave him a sour look as if he'd asked her for a kidney but handed over a pencil.

Butchie had never used a microfilm machine before and it made him dizzy, but he learned to avert his eyes to keep the nausea from making him upchuck right there in the library carrel. The librarian told him the Enterprise's archives had recently been digitized. He started too far back when a less politically correct time—or maybe one less squeamish—noted the Brockton deceased beneath a single, matter-of-fact word followed by a full stop: DEAD. A couple decades later, the list of the Brockton deceased were sentimentalized with favorite hobbies like watching Red Sox games and cheering for the Patriots and fatuous clichés about how they would never hesitate to give anyone who needed it the shirt off their backs.

Butchie found him even though he himself was a boy when he overheard his father lamenting his cousin Angelo's wayward daughter. Apparently she was a "slattern" and his father blamed her neglect for the death of her illegitimate child from the flu, which was bad that year. Butchie was seven and stayed home all week from it. His dad refused to tell Butchie what slattern meant. He'd found him under Parmentieri, the name never Americanized, despite the same ancestor arriving on that coffin ship in Boston Harbor back in 1856. His great-grandfather always blamed an illiterate Irish cop as the reason for it. The boy was Butchie's age. Perfect.

Butchie decided to quit while he was ahead. He had another minor item of business to attend to: Nino Frabutt.

"Odraye been in touch with you?"

"No, I ain't seen him in weeks. Not since last time you called. What's up?"

Good old Nino, singing to his own sheet music no matter what the symphony is playing.

"When's the last time you saw him?" Butchie asked.

"I don't remember. That time with you, I think. No maybe a couple, three days afterward. He came around working asking for you. You know how black dudes say 'askin' like 'axin''? Cracks me up."

"Why was he looking for me?"

"I don't know," Nino said. "He was acting weird, like. I said, 'Odraye, man, what up? You're wandering around here like you're lookin' for the lost head of John the Baptist, and he stares at me like I'm hiding something from him. Gave me the creeps. What's goin' on with you two?"

"Nothing," Butchie said. "We'll bump into each other one

of these days." Butchie thought of the bad guys arriving on the noon train.

"I got something belongs to him. If you see him or hear from him, mention that, OK?"

"Will do. There's an MMA match coming up at Rox Stadium. You wanna go?"

"Can't. Got things to do."

"Hey, I heard something the other night at the Club. Is it true?"

"Every word of it," Butchie replied.

"Ho-oly shit."

"See you, Nino."

Telling the truth came with a kick: he'd been lying so long to so many people it felt good for a change.

"You sure you want to do this?"

"I'm sure," Butchie said.

The salesman had already run a check on the license and registration. Butchie's credit wasn't an issue. He was letting himself get reamed in the trade.

Butchie handed him the keys to the Jeep after he parked beside it. "I just need to clear out the junk in the back," he told the man.

"You want some help?"

"No, thanks, I can get it," Butchie replied. "Got my flathead right here." Butchie wagged the screwdriver in his hand.

"You came prepared," the guy said. His name was Irish, something like Corky.

"You never know what you'll find waiting for you," Butchie told him.

"Looks like my wife's car," he joked, watching Butchie open the gate. "She can move into her back seat with all the stuff she carries around. I tell her, 'A clean car is a happy car,' but she don't listen worth shit."

"That's me, too," Butchie said. "I like having my stuff with me."

"Hey, whatever floats your boat," the man said and walked away in the direction of the shack he had for an office.

Butchie put the money bags in the trunk and piled as much of the other belongings on top as he could and still close the lid. He carried the rest to the dumpster and tossed everything in. He'd made the salesman's day, that was for sure. He'd practically given away his Wrangler with 5,000 miles for his new wheels, a 2008 Saturn Vue with 92,000 miles and three hundred dollars cash. The salesman must have sprayed it with a shot of some lavender deodorant before Butchie test-drove it a couple blocks. A whiff of onions from a McDonald's bag under the seat lingered as he got back in and drove off.

Butchie drove to his motel and parked a distance away. He needed a shower. His body had stopped perspiring and his last piss came out neon yellow. He worried he was damaging his kidneys, not hydrating enough in the heat, not to mention the assaults on his liver with the alcohol. He lit a cigarette and smoked.

He gulped two bottles of water while staring through the windshield. A new habit: surveille everything before you get out. Left, right, corners, trees, behind most of all. The parking lot looked the same.

Farther down the lot, heat shimmer distorted his vision. He never got out of his car without scoping the environment first nowadays, the new situational awareness becoming a habit like the cigarettes scorching his lungs. He watched some people arrive at the motel. He'd discovered his new residence was a trysting place for weekend couples and cheating spouses. Some high-school kids had rented the room next to his and used it for partying. He'd barely slept last night. He tensed every time he heard people walking past his room.

He'd swung by his apartment and collected his mail. Some utility bills, the letter from his department informing him he was being terminated for cause.

High-school kids in punk clothing and dyed hair walked across the lot. Fuckin' great, another party, Butchie thought.

One stopped a few feet from Butchie's room and turned around, as if he'd forgotten something, and walked back the way he came. Butchie went back to reading the letter again, even the commas, in case there was a mistake. "Unauthorized use of city vehicles," some dates noted, including That Day, cited as cause for termination. It didn't carry Asaro's signature but Butchie felt his influence all over it despite the formal language. The last paragraph involved his appeal and a bunch of codes and numbers, which he ignored. Well, that was that.

He looked up and saw another kid, this one wearing military boots and a black tee with the word THIEF in a patch sewn across his back. He was inked up, both arms, another craze Butchie spurned. Now it made him feel like an old man out of touch with youth. You couldn't keep track of the phases anymore. It was as if life had sped up and was rushing toward some apocalyptic conclusion that a few were in on while the majority of sheep continued to graze on the hillside. Until recently, he had been one of those sheep, mindlessly chewing the cud under the eye of the butcher.

The boy with the tatts and combat boots headed toward the lobby but glanced in the direction of Butchie's room. Something else about him looked suspicious; he was olive-complected, not Italian but Hispanic. When he turned around, Butchie saw the ink of gothic lettering on his forehead.

No high schooler, an MS-13 member. Suddenly, two more youths of the same size and look appeared out of nowhere and joined the first boy, who'd come back into sight. The four of them bunched up around Butchie's door, one leaning over it, and in no time the room was opened. All four piled in.

Butchie watched, his focus intent on the door and the window where drapes covered every inch of glass. He thought of taking off, but forced himself to stay. He had plenty of time if they came out and spotted him. They were inside for fifteen minutes. No lights were turned on as far as he could tell from his distance. Then one shaved head appeared in the open doorway, looking both ways, like a fledgling peering over a nest. In rapid order, they all left single file and did a fast-walk across the lot. Butchie heard an engine start up. A gray SUV passed him. Sun glare reflected kaleidoscope imagery across the windshield, so he couldn't see if all four were inside.

He waited several more minutes before he went inside his room. It was gutted more than ransacked. Unlike the chaos of his apartment where things were scattered in a rage, this was more a professional job with drawers left open and everything searched. The mattresses were slit, same with the pillows. Even the vents were removed and checked. Looking for the money. If he'd been there, they'd have used their knives on him and whatever else they carried for persuasion. MS-13 liked machetes. They'd have spent days inside with him, if necessary.

Butchie felt numb. They could have been hired by Odraye or even Hoyt for all he knew. Or they could be freelancers who'd heard the rumors and picked up his trail like dogs on a scent. A guy driving around in a cherry Jeep for all to see like some open-mouthed buffoon. And not just any guy but a guy rumored to have taken an old woman's earnings over a lifetime of scrimping and saving.

He gathered up his clothes, shoes, and shaving gear. His duffel bag was slit across the bottom, so he took a sheet from the bed and threw everything into it; he folded the corners like a giant hobo sack, carried it out to his Saturn and tossed it on the passenger seat.

He stopped by the lobby to turn in his key. The clerk told him he couldn't get a refund for the days he wouldn't be staying because he'd been on "the weekly rate."

"Keep it," Butchie said. "There's been some damage. You can take it out of my credit card."

"Fucking-A, we will."

Butchie parked on School Street behind City Hall, a red-brick gabled Victorian structure with some Romanesque touches and a massive rounded turret. When his dad used to take him downtown, he imagined being up there with John Wayne, shooting down on Apaches and defending the women and children. He didn't know when it had gone from defending them to robbing from them, but somewhere along the way he fell short of his childhood fantasies.

The City Clerk's Office had the same three pleasant women staffing it. One of them was his high-school classmate who hated him because she blamed him for abetting her husband's adultery. It was true. He'd given so little thought to it, what that meant to her. She didn't avoid him or give him the malocchio whenever he had business there. They'd even spoken about the next class reunion. She was a gum-chewing, platinum blonde in those days but smarter than she acted. He wondered how many women like her discarded the bimbo mask once they had jobs and families to care for. Courtship no longer started with a capital c for any of them in the wake of their teenaged years; formal mating was deader than Julius Caesar. Spill your guts on social media, dating sites, make cute duck faces for the boys and get a good glam shot with plenty of boobs on display.

"Yo, Marianne."

"Hey, Butchie."

Two uncomfortable minutes of catching up.

He filled out the one-page form and paid the fee. In the box that asked him for the reason for wanting to obtain the certificate, he started to put Get Lost but changed it to Genealogy, hoping he'd spelled it correctly.

Marianne took the form and read it in front of him. When she looked at him, he thought he detected a sly smile. Jesus, is it that obvious what I'm doing? She came back with a Xerox of the birth certificate.

"You want it certified? It'll cost ya five dollars more," she said.

"Sure, let's go for broke," he said.

Butchie was holding the Saturn door open, gazing around the parking lot for a last check when the bullet sizzled the air next to his head. His flinch was involuntary and wouldn't have mattered if the bullet struck. He registered the carom off a metal guardrail, saw the spark.

He threw himself down to the asphalt and rolled into whatever shelter was afforded by the vehicle's front bumper; he lay there trying to squeeze his body under the grill, panting, afraid to rise, terrified to be visible for the next shot. He couldn't see anything but the iridescent puddle of coolant near a tire. He was aware of an engine block ticking once, a sound his fear rarefied into a looming threat. Someone nearby, sitting in a car, watching, holding a weapon on me right now . . . he scrunched his head lower into his chin like a baby turtle among seagulls. Calmer, he realized it had to be a rifle and it had to be a distance away.

His mind raced, hesitated.

Get up, go, go, go!

"You OK down there, fella?"

An older man in a Hawaiian shirt with blue parrots stared down at him. He was carrying papers in his hand and slightly bent at the waist just staring at Butchie.

For a terrifying split-second Butchie thought he might be the shooter coming to finish him off and his sphincter muscle tightened.

"I'm. . . I'm fine, I'm OK," Butchie said, his voice squeaky, a pre-pubescent male whose sac hadn't dropped. He rose on shaky legs, a wheat silo about to topple but steadied himself against the hood of his car.

"Just, uh, checking for an oil leak."

"I thought maybe you was havin' a heart attack or something like that but you're way too young."

He had a grizzled chin from a bad shave and a bristly moustache with pointed ends like tiny gray flames.

"See this?"

He opened his shirt and revealed a white jagged scar that looked like a centipede beneath his thick gray chest hairs. "Triple bypass—can you believe it? I'm only fifty-seven."

Butchie's own father's age when he died of bleeding ulcers. An omen? Butchie had gone from no faith in anything to a belief in everything—ghosts, omens, and karma, all in a single week. Cars turned into the lot. A group of women giggling and chatting appeared from the same doors he'd come through moments ago. Normal was restored like water finding its equilibrium back as if the shot that just missed him had never been fired. A flock of pigeons erupted from a nearby rooftop and flew over. Butchie winced.

"You sure you're OK?"

"I'm sure."

God help me, I'll be praying in the middle of the street next.

He spotted a newspaper in the man's other hand.

"Sir, could I buy that paper off you? The vending machine was empty on my way out," Butchie said, brushing grit off the front of his shirt.

"This? Heck, you can have it," the man said. "Nothin' much in it anyway. Buncha thieves in city hall, same as ever."

Not all of them in city hall, Butchie thought.

He watched the man walk off, thought of his father again and got in his car sitting low behind the steering wheel. He knew he could never feel safe anywhere again.

He flipped through the pages looking for more information on the murders and found what he was looking for—more than he was looking for.

Forshey was quoted throughout one article, which included a couple paragraphs and photos of John Bello and the reporter's interview with Leotis Marsten's mother. A sentence grabbed his eye: "The Bellos' oldest son "Johnny" (Giovanni) Bello claimed his family's money had been stolen by thieves and he hoped the Brockton police department would help them recover it. 'My mother slaved for that money for fifty years,' he said to this reporter; 'she didn't deserve to have this happen.'"

He was near the end of the piece when his own name jumped out at him: "Former housing inspector Tommaso Parmenter has been named as 'a person of interest.' Parmenter's employment was recently terminated by Brockton Housing Department."

No mention of Odraye Suggs, the last person to see Leotis

alive. Cops held back information from the public. If Forshey had him bagged up, he couldn't keep a lid on it for long. Odraye would turn state's evidence on Butchie in a heartbeat if he could get away with it.

No, that's not it, Butchie thought.

Forshey released his name as a way to put on the pressure—to get him to come in and talk first. The tiny red LED light on his phone recorder at home had semaphored full capacity. Three from friends, basically asking him, What-the-fuck? Six were from that same reporter from The Enterprise and three were from Det. Forshey all starting the same way: "How ya doin', Butchie?" Or "Hey, Butchie, I was wondering. . ." followed by a pretty-please request for him to come down to the precinct to answer "just a couple more questions—you know, unburden yourself a little."

Unburden myself of my freedom and the money both, right, Forshey? He can kiss my ass in the crack. . .

Everything reshaped itself around normality: cars parked in rows, telephone poles, signs with arrows and floor numbers listing an A to Z directory from the Auditor to the Office of Weights and Measures. Others told you where to pay bills, report distracted drivers or discarded needles. A back lot of a New England city behind a municipal building replete with pigeons and a couple mourning doves trilling their three flute notes. Norman Rockwell, not Salvador Dali. Yet a sniper had taken two shots at him and missed. Not Odraye, Butchie thought. He'd want to be up close when he took my head off. He shielded his eyes from the sun trying to see where a sniper could hide out there beyond the back parking lot. Weeds grew up around cement-block foundations. Some sway-backed garages, old brownstones slated to be demolished next spring for the new annex. Hoyt, he decided, using his own method of communication to send him a message, reminding him he was still out there.

CHAPTER 20

The unmarked behind Butchie wasn't trying to hide, either. It made him realize how badly Forshey must want him. Twenty-four-hour surveillance was usually reserved for the worst cases, the kidnappings and the terrorists. Brockton PD had probably pulled in the Commonwealth's state police for the job. He'd seen a few vans with the aerial whips and Boston news logos in his random excursions about town. Maybe it was some instinct from the basal ganglia, that clump of nerves at the stump of the neck vertebrae telling him to keep moving, motion is good, movement saves lives. He didn't know. He was in a waiting game.

Butchie's next budget motel was a step lower on the socioeconomic ladder. Empty booze bottles lined the walkway in the mornings, and there was plenty of action after dark. Cars pulling in throughout the night, lots of headboard-bumping against the back wall. A woman's steady trill—a rippling soprano O-O-O reaching through the vent to twist his entrails and remind him of his celibacy.

The insomnia was relieved by a couple hours of deep black sleep until just before dawn. Scary, threatening images—just amorphous black cloud shapes without faces—tumbled out of his dreams like clowns out of a circus Volkswagen.

He sat at the edge of the bed and smoked. The nicotine habit accrued daily, a monster of his own making, but he felt he needed something to calm the nerves while he waited. Waited, for what? Butchie asked himself in the mirror—for Odraye Suggs to jump out of the hedges like some lion on the savanna? In an odd trick of his mind, he didn't fear a sniper's bullet punching a hole through his brain at some odd moment when he was out in the open. It just wasn't Hoyt's style, not devious enough.

Butchie fetched the paper from the vending machine in the lobby. The clerk behind the desk reminded him of his former place: the same bored indifference to people, a whey-faced contempt for the customer who dared to interrupt his nighttime video game with a question about ice or where the vending machine was located. Before this, Butchie had assumed all chain motels were run by Indians with beaming smiles and polite sing-song enquiries about his "pleasant stay," generally oblivious to the real purpose as an adulterous liaison with a married woman from work or one he'd encountered through his night life. He was seeing a new reality in America that had always been there in the seething hatred of the unskilled laboring class.

Butchie drove to his apartment and found a 14-day notice to quit taped to the door, still leaning against its frame. His landlord used a thin sisal rope wrapped back and forth between the rails several times like a drunken spiderweb to prevent anyone from climbing the front steps. Butchie glanced at the notice; he'd seen dozens like these and knew the wording almost by heart. He recognized the constable's signature, too. He'd seen him in the bars around town.

Butchie decided it wasn't worth another look inside, but he had to check his phone messages in case Neecie, for some reason, decided to call him at home. She sometimes did that when they were having spats. She didn't want him answering his cell and interrupting her "Shakespearean soliloquy," as he called it, recalling a term from high-school English class. She always said it let her get her thoughts in order. It endeared her to him but he never let her know that.

He stepped over the clutter, a maze of debris left intact since his last visit. No message from Neecie but two from her brother.

"Hey, asshole, you don't learn, do you? I told you to leave her alone."

"Butchie, listen, sorry about that. I was upset. I spoke to Neecie. She told me how she feels about you. How about we get together over a beer tonight? I'd like to talk to you and get all this crap between us out of the way once and for good. What do you say? The Club, tonight, about ten. See you then."

Anthony, the peacemaker. Butchie was suspicious but hopeful at the same time. If what he said about Neecie's feelings for him were true, he had a chance. He didn't want to blow it. It wouldn't hurt to see the arrogant prick and find out. Anthony wouldn't be able to bring his tagalong biker pals with him to the Fratellanza anyway. Butchie could count on more people liking him than Anthony any day of the week, which, he realized, wasn't much of a testimonial to his own character.

Butchie collected his mail and saw the letter from the city; his namesake, that long-dead, father's cousin's daughter's dead son's birth certificate: Tommaso Parmentieri, born in Brockton in 1984, died in Boston, 1993. Now he had the death certificate with the child's social security number noted on it, the birth certificate, and all he needed was a second piece of identification.

Butchie grabbed a bunch of bills lying on the table where he'd tossed them from his last visit and drove to the East Brockton Public Library on Kingman. He had been there once before. He signed up for one of the half-hour computer stations and waited until he was called. He didn't recognize any of the women or the one man on duty that day. Andy, the technical geek who had helped him on that one previous visit, said he only worked late afternoons.

Butchie printed up some mailing labels for the address of a flophouse hotel on the same street as his current motel. He pasted these over the envelopes and inside addresses of his mail and Xeroxed them both, thinking three sets should do it. He paid for his xeroxes at the desk and mentioned he'd recently lost his wallet—Gosh darn it!—with all his cards and driver's license, and would she please issue him another library card? She would.

He had plenty of time to get to the Plymouth County RMV

Bureau. The obese woman in the print dress at the counter grumbled about the lateness of the time.

"I though you closed at four-thirty," Butchie said.

"We close at three-thirty on Fridays. See the times on the window?" She pointed a fat wrist encircled by loops of turquoise bracelet that made Butchie think of a python climbing a tree. She meant the pebbled glass window he'd ignored on his way inside.

Butchie flashed his little-boy smile Neecie always said was cute "as a bug's ass" and offered to bake a cake for her wedding; she smiled and grudgingly agreed to process the form.

Thank you, Jesus. . .

She asked another woman working on her computer to show him to the photo booth, where she snapped his picture. Ten minutes later, two minutes to closing time, Butchie had his state ID card.

"Can you really bake a wedding cake?"

He turned around in the doorway. It was the same woman who first met him at the desk.

"Not only bake one," Butchie said, "but one that'll taste like an angel pissing on your tongue."

He drove the Saturn recklessly, punishing it for replacing his beloved Jeep, and hoping to get there just as their work day was ending; in fact, he wanted a hurry-up job for this card, one they'd be eager to do and get him gone. He had all the right papers now, but it was crucial to get the Social Security card. He didn't know how many days he had left in Brockton with all this shit swirling above his head like dirt sucked up in a tornado's vortex that hovered and came down all at once. No guarantees now.

He also felt like a shit doing this to a distant relative he'd never met but said he'd light a candle in church for the dead boy Tommaso as recompense—that was a big word in Fr. Montesanti's vocabulary back in the day.

The unmarked swung in behind him three car lengths back.

"That's OK, boys, stay close," Butchie said to the rearview

mirror. "I'm running with wolves now. I can't afford to trip."

Three missed messages.

Det. Forshey. "Hey, Butchie, I was wondering—"

Erased. "Wonder that, Forshey."

Hoyt. "Anybody can hit a standing target in broad daylight from one hundred yards. It takes skill to miss."

Erased. "Fuck you, Hoyt."

Nino. "I got a call from Odraye last night, about two in the morning. I told him what you said. He sounded strange. He said he'd catch up with you real soon. . .That's what he said, like that. . . Are you in trouble?"

Am I ever—

"I think it's for the best," Asaro said, nodding, sagely considering things from both perspectives.

"I do, too, Dan," Butchie said. "I think I was. . . losing my grip there for a while. I'd forgotten what's important in life."

Asaro made that irritating tent with his fingers while Butchie stood in front of his desk, looking around at the framed certificates of appreciation on one wall, the colored photos of his wife and kids on the other. Asaro the professional man balanced by Asaro the family man. He suddenly unlocked his fingers and swept up the keys to the garage and locker Butchie had placed there, as if fearing Butchie might change his mind and appeal the decision.

"I think it's for the best, don't you?" Asaro repeated, eager to get rid of him.

Butchie smiled and suddenly lunged forward, his right hand outstretched, a shabby imitation of the Rocky Punch.

Asaro reared back in his seat, the springs creaking beneath his weight, and attempted to cover his fright from Butchie's pouncing like that by clearing his throat. The supervisor had done a PowerPoint to the staff titled "Signs of Workplace Violence" just two weeks ago.

"No hard feelings," Butchie said.

Asaro shook Butchie's hand. The color bloomed in his cheeks like mismatched rosettes.

"Good luck, Butchie."

"Be seeing you."

"Any plans?"

Butchie hesitated at the door, thinking it over.

"As a matter of fact, I do have plans."

He shut the door and headed for the elevator and punched the button for the garage.

"Hey, Butch, you comin' back to work, you lazy wop?"

Pete Nixon, maintenance, back from his three-week vacation in Hialeah where he spent every day at the track betting the greyhounds. He still owed Butchie a hundred over the Sox-Yanks doubleheader a month back.

"Hey, Petey, I need to borrow the arc welder. Is it back here somewhere in this shithole?"

"No, I left it upstairs in Asaro's office. I'm gonna cut him a new asshole. Of course, it's back here, you mutt. Got a fresh oxygen tank. What else you need?"

"Just some tools," Butchie said. "I'll grab them on the way. You want me to sign out?"

"Naw, fuck it," Petey said. "Take what you need."

Pete wheeled the tanks out for him and handed him the welder's helmet.

"What all you got goin' here, Butchie?"

"Better you don't know, Pete. I'll see you."

"Look, about that money I owe you—"

"Keep it," Butchie said. "Buy your kid a toy instead."

"Damn, thanks, Butchie. I lost my ass on the dogs down there."

It was a different kind of dog Butchie had in mind just then. The kind that returneth to its vomit.

City workers had placed sawhorses around the entire Bello store. Yellow crime scene tape flapped across the front of the building. The looky-loos had stopped gawking at it by now. Pedestrian traffic crisscrossed the street, mostly single black males, or young girls, white and black, pushing brown babies in strollers. All else looked the same—no serious demolition effort yet. He noted a few small piles of loose brick some workers had gathered off the sidewalk and left behind. He banished the image of standing inside with Odraye and Leotis, seeing that sledgehammer rise up over Suggs' shoulder like some yokel at a country fair with a mallet trying to ring the bell.

Butchie wished he had the city truck with him in case any cruisers went by, but that would be too much to ask for. He hoped Petey didn't mention anything that got back to Asaro.

Bolt cutters snapped the lock. He replaced the missing Condemned placard with a new one from his locker. He wheeled the welding tanks inside and took a survey of the rooms to be sure. When he found the right spot, he lifted the tanks off and used it as a two-wheeler to haul the fridge to the other side against a wall where the drywall had rotted completely away from rain. The brick mortar flaked off at a touch. He eyeballed the fridge and mentally measured off the position and number of bricks he'd have to remove. Once that was done, he built up around the hole to disguise the damage. He'd have to check outside to make sure the height and reach were good.

Butchie knew shielded metal and TIG, but it had been awhile since he struck an arc. He placed the mask on his head and set to work. It didn't have to be perfect and in the dim lighting; it was feasible no one would notice.

An hour later, he had finished. He discarded the metal racks and placed the two white garbage bags side by side inside the refrigerator on top of the plexiglass divider where the fruits went into one bin and the vegetables in the other. He secured the refrigerator to the wall with bolts.

He gathered his equipment and put everything inside the trunk or tossed onto the back seat. One more check of the outside wall to be sure. He looked to see if any pedestrians approached. Traffic was sparse when he stepped around the corner and walked over the slimy leaves blown against the side of the building. He'd risk that much. He had to be sure of the distance or it was all for nothing.

It looked good. His arm extended all the way inside and reached the plate he'd set up against the back of the refrigerator.

He replaced the lock on the front door with one of his own.

Back at the garage, Butchie's luck held out. Pete was alone again. Butchie wheeled the tanks over and dropped the tools on the work bench.

"That was fast," Pete said. "Get 'er done?"

"I don't know," Butchie said. "It's up to the gods now."

"Hunh?"

"So long, Petey."

Butchie went back to his motel. He was certain it wouldn't be long now, but he couldn't predict exactly what would happen or the order in which it would happen. He figured he'd better eat, although he had little appetite. His pants were loose on his hips and he saw ribs he hadn't seen since he pumped iron in his twenties.

This place had a radio instead of a television set or else the one for the room was either stolen or out for repairs. He saw two large elbow braces lying in the top drawer of the chest on top of a brochure featuring a list of soft-porn films available for guests.

His mind wandered, he let it go where it chose—some good memories, some bad. Mostly disconnected thoughts that inevitably wound back to the last week and all that happened. He would never stop seeing Leotis Marsten on the floor or Delores on the bed. He tried to remember Neecie in their better times. He kept checking his watch. He must have nodded off a few times because the room got dark on its own.

He heard children outside somewhere playing. That was a pleasant thought to close his eyes on again and so he did. He was walking in a garden enjoying the scents of verbena and hollyhock. The petals of a tulip tree were scattered about the lawn; stepping on them, enjoying the squishy feel of them under his feet, accelerated into pacing, then marching. When the children's voices grew louder, he stopped. They were approaching from the perimeter hedges of the garden—a loose pack, howling, and up close he could see their blue faces: MS-13 gangsters with machetes, coming at him in a rush. . . He flung himself off the bed and came up standing, crouched, with the revolver aimed at the door. No one there.

"I was dreaming," Butchie said to the empty room.

He checked the time: 8:47.

He called Bittaker's.

"Bobby, that guy who's been looking for me, the one you said has been coming in every night at the same time. Is he in tonight?"

"Yeah, he's in here now. The big bastard, the weirdo with the head full of girlie curls. Look, I told you if you're in trouble with this dude, I can help."

"I appreciate it, but no."

"Your funeral," Bobby said.

Not yet. . .

He called Neecie. It went to voicemail.

It was a hunch. Ever since he'd switched cars, Hoyt had taken to scoping out Butchie's watering holes, chatting up his friends.

He hit the number for Bittaker's Bar from his directory. This was going to be slicker than cat shit on a marble floor if he pulled it off. The odds were against it, but with Odraye on the agenda, he decided to go for a twofer rather than face Hoyt on his own turf at a time he chose.

"Tell him I'm on my way to the Fratellanza, Bobby. Give him directions if he doesn't know where it is."

Time to go see what Anthony had to say to him. Butchie didn't know why he felt that excitable surge in his belly. This wasn't part of the plan—or was it? Sometimes the gods took over and you did what they said—or else.

Anthony was sitting astride his Fat Boy when Butchie pulled into the lot.

"Hey, where's your Jeep?"

"I traded it in."

"Looks like you traded down, way down," Anthony said. "That's a real piece of shit."

"Let's talk about, Neecie."

"No, I don't think so. But there's someone here who does want to talk to you. Ciao, fuckface."

Anthony throttled his machine and left a patch of rubber behind.

"Hello, Butchie." Odraye's bass hummed behind him in the shadows between two SUVs.

"Look, I know you're pissed," Butchie said, turning around.

"How can you tell?"

"The way you just spoke." Each syllable drawn and quartered. What came last—the beheading? His head on a pole somewhere.

"I would have thought it was something else a little more important than that, Butchie. Like how you stole my money and ran off."

"Odraye, I haven't run anywhere. I've been here all this time. I'm trying to figure out how we can do this and get clear."

"Shut. . .Your. . . Mouth. . . Bitch."

Good. Odraye was too far away to land a punch, Butchie thought.

He had his hand around the butt of the revolver and had it up to the barrel against his flesh when he felt Odraye's hand locked on his with an iron grip.

Oh Christ! Don't squeeze the trigger while it's pointing at my cock—

Butchie saw the gun free itself from his waist and get tucked inside Odraye's. It couldn't have been done with any less wasted motion than if they'd practiced it for weeks. Like ballet. He knew he was in trouble when Odraye ducked into a fighter's crouch and stepped forward, Odraye's right foot splitting his own legs, to land a solid punch to the side of Butchie's head.

So that's what it feels like, Butchie thought, spitting blood to the pavement. A strand of ropy drool stayed attached to his lip. He sat up and spat a gob of blood-flecked phlegm. Odraye stood where he was when he threw the punch. In the hazy light of the Club's parking lot, he seemed frozen like Marciano in Champions Park.

Butchie tried to get up but wound up doing a face plant into the concrete. That seemed funny for some reason and he giggled. Jesus Christ, I'm concussed, he thought and tried to rope his mind back into place by an act of will.

"Get the fuck up, motherfucker. I am going to punch your brains in."

No sadistic enunciating but no anger either. Just a flat prediction.

"Money," Butchie said. "I have the money. You can. . . have. . ."

He was forced to lean over and spit out more blood. The side of his face was swollen and the cut inside his mouth rubbed against his teeth when he spoke making it difficult to talk.

". . . all the money. Yours. All of it," Butchie said and stood up. "I'm tired of it, tired of all you crazy motherfuckers."

"I am still going to beat your narrow white ass," Odraye said.

"Let me show. . . show you the money, where it is," Butchie said. It came out in sputters, a pathetic whine, not the manly bravado he'd intended. Nothing at all like the strong, silent Cooper of High Noon. Hell, I'm not even good enough for Lloyd Bridges's part. I'm a lowlife Brockton shitheels dealing with scum worse than I am.

Odraye was suddenly in front of him looming like a thundercloud. Butchie closed his eyes, not wanting to see it coming. When it didn't land, he opened his eyes to see a single ham-sized, scarred fist tensed in front of his nose. The air seemed to vibrate all around his face from the sheer inertia of that cocked fist. Behind the third-base dugout once, he'd seen the bat jump out of David Ortiz's hand quivering in mid-air after a towering shot over the Green Monster.

"Where is it, you fuck?"

"Bello's store," Butchie said. "It's in there."

He remained stock-still, afraid to take even a small step backwards.

"You lying sack of dog shit, I'll kill you if you're lying to me." Odraye said it in a single breath.

"I had nowhere else to put it," Butchie replied. "If the cops found it on me, I'd be slammed in jail. This way, it's like it was never taken, see?"

"Let's go get it," Odraye said. "God, I am so sick of you, Butchie."

Gripping Butchie's shoulder, Odraye pushed him ahead toward the Saturn.

"You were going to shoot me with this gun, weren't you, Butchie?"

Butchie felt the barrel pressed against the nape of his neck.

"You were going to kill me," Butchie said.

"I might still kill you yet."

He shoved Butchie inside and climbed into the driver's seat.

"Can you drive standard shift?" Butchie asked.

"What the fuck," Odraye said.

Lightning didn't strike twice—mainly because Odraye had the agility of a cat and the Vue was easier to make the switch. Odraye pressed what felt like a sumo wrestler's weight into him, crushing him against the seat back and manhandling him into the driver's seat without the fatal miscue that had changed Maurice Jelks's destiny. His tiny Pico Beretta rubbed against his ankle where he'd strapped it in with three rubber bands.

"Why didn't you say so in the first place, you fuck?"

"Sorry," Butchie said.

"Drive. Stay five miles under the speed limit. No stupid shit or you get a bullet."

Butchie timed it so he hit all the red lights without alerting Suggs. He wanted to provide plenty of time for the cops to keep them in sight. Traffic was light on all the major roads despite the weekend nightlife crowd.

"Butchie," Odraye said, his tone lighter now, bantering, "I just might let you keep some of that money."

"That's mighty white of you," Butchie said.

"What did you say?"

"Don't go all Black-Lives-Matter on me, Odraye. The money's there but I'm the only one who can find it. You need me. The cops are looking all over town for you. Be smart."

"You talk too much, you dago fucker. That was my big mistake. Listening to your bool-shit about 'we got to clean the money,' 'we got to find the right bank,' all that smoke you blew up my ass. That money will spend just fine where I'm gonna be at."

"Oh? And where's that going to be, Odraye?"

"Corner of Fuck-You and Kiss-My-Ass. None a your got-damn fuck-ass business."

"OK."

"Shut the fuck up right now, asshole!"

"OK."

The barrel jabbed Butchie in his swollen jaw.

"Fuck, that really hurts, Odraye."

"I meant it to hurt, you dickhead."

"I gotta spit some blood out, OK?"

Butchie started to roll down the window. This time the barrel went into his neck and he heard the snick of the double-action trigger. A few more pounds of pressure. . .

"Swallow it," Odraye demanded. "You are aggravatin' me something fierce, white boy."

Butchie knew it was a calculated risk, a moonshot. Odraye talking, however, was better than Odraye punching and stomping him to death. He wanted him thinking about the money, not about Butchie's treachery. Every mile back to Montebello was stretched out in taffy-pull time.

No more clock time, Butchie thought. It's a new dimension I'm existing in.

Butchie saw the tan Crown Royal, giving him an adrenalin surge all its own. He forced himself not to stare in the rearview. Odraye fiddled with the radio, cursed it for having so many "shitkicker" stations.

Odraye sounded appeased at last. He prattled at Butchie in

his mumbling, guttural manner, half-talking to himself. A big cat about to feast. Butchie felt Odraye gain confidence, grow happy now the money was finally in his reach. The rage had subsided for the moment, but Butchie knew it would come roaring back once he wrapped his mitts around those wads of bills and felt it safe to put the finishing touch on his own plan. Then Butchie might not see the KO coming but he would be as useful to Odraye as those single-use plastic grocery bags. Odraye's intentions were as subtle as a showroom full of coffins.

Butchie saw his move in Odraye's greed. He wheedled, pleaded for Odraye to kick him "a few bucks."

"You realize I lost my job, man. I got fired because of you."

"You think I give a fuck, Butchie? Fuck you."

Harsh but not the fuck-you-I'll-kill-you tone earlier.

"I need to start over, man" Butchie pleaded.

"You be lucky if I let you breathe air. I'm tired of your bullshit and lies. That money better be there. I can't believe you took it back there, you dumb ass motherfucker!"

"I had no choice, Odraye, after you tore my place up looking for it."

"What you expect me to do, man?"

Keep jabbering away, Butchie thought, and I'll keep playing the fool.

"About goddamn time, you slow-assed bitch. Park around the corner."

Butchie pulled the Saturn around the corner but kept going.

"Stop the fuckin' car!"

The barrel of the gun slapped him on his sore jaw.

"Easy, Odraye. I'm parking down a little ways to get out of the light."

"Those people in that house see us, I'll kill your ass right here," Odraye said.

Butchie needed to stall for time; something wasn't right. He hadn't seen the cop car for the last five miles. Maybe they weren't coming.

"You better have bolt cutters in the trunk," Odraye said, "or else you're gonna chew that lock off with your teeth."

"Don't need them," Butchie said. "Got a key in my pocket. Housing inspector, remember?"

"I thought you said you was fired."

Butchie leaned over to spit blood and chips of tooth on the floor.

"Nasty motherfucker, you."

"Can I get out now?"

"I'll have my hand on your belt and don't forget this." Odraye waved the gun at him.

"That's your gun, isn't it?" Butchie asked him. "Not Maurice's."

"So what? I gave it to Diz and he said he dropped it."

"He did. I picked it up."

Butchie couldn't explain it. In his senior year at Brockton, he drag-raced some guy in a '90 Camaro Coupe at four in the morning. They were doing eighty on North Montello coming up on the Avon intersection when the other guy dropped back. Butchie watched the Camaro disappear in the rearview mirror wondering if he'd had engine trouble. Too late, he saw two parked cars in the road on opposite sides. Butchie held his breath and blew between the cars with an inch to spare on either side. He told Neecie about it at school the next morning and she said he'd experienced a satori, a word she'd glommed onto from her geography teacher, a "hunk" he was jealous of.

"What's that?"

"It's, like, when you understand something you didn't know before," she'd said.

"You killed them," Butchie said. "You killed all three of them."

Odraye sighed and sat back against the seat. He slapped the barrel of the gun into his fist.

"That's not real smart of you, Butchie. To say something like that to me, is it?"

"I thought Jelks was a friend."

"We did some business."

"Delores?"

"Bitch couldn't keep her mouth shut," Odraye said. "She had to go one way or the other."

"Quinnel Jones, he just happened to be in the wrong place at the wrong time, I suppose?"

Odraye shrugged: one more slice off a cut loaf.

"Now let's go, real slow, no sudden moves, no talking. Get the key out and do it slow," Odraye ordered him.

Butchie showed him the key and told him there was a flashlight in the glovebox. He pulled the door latch and got out. True to his word, Odraye's thick fingers gripped the back of his belt. He stood by the car while Odraye shifted over to his side and stood up next to him.

"Move it."

Odraye nudged a sawhorse aside with his leg and gripped Butchie's bicep with his free hand. Butchie fumbled with the key until Odraye jammed the gun into the back of his head.

"Open it."

He didn't think Odraye would kill him right there in front of the store, but the man had a reptile's blood and he wasn't sure.

They were inside. Scratching noises on the wooden floor suggested the mice were aware of them.

"Take the light," Odraye said. "Keep it pointed at the floor unless I say different. Fuck with me, Butchie, and you'll die on this shitty floor."

"I understand."

They walked in tandem to the far back of the house, Odraye's hand on Butchie's shoulder, the barrel placed in the middle of his back.

"What the fuck. Where is it?"

"Workers must have moved it to the other side. They're tearing this place down tomorrow. It's over there, see? Against that wall."

"Why in the fuck did they padlock it for?"

"Who knows?"

"Get to it," Odraye said.

Butchie snapped the padlock with heavy-duty bolt cutters. His flashlight beam shone on the two bags.

"There it is. Your share and mine," Butchie said.

"Keep dreaming, shithead. Pull a stack out."

"What for? It's all there," Butchie said.

"I want to check, see you didn't wrap a twenty around a wad of ones or play me with some ghetto trick."

Butchie reached inside and grabbed one wad of bills and handed it to Odraye.

"Take one from that stack and that other one," Odraye commanded. "Grab from the middle."

"Spread 'em out and put the light on them. Now, I see one phony bill or one cut-out piece of newspaper, you get a bullet right here, understand me, Butchie?"

"Understood," he said. I'm getting that bullet in the head anyway. . .

His beam flickered over the wads of money, all tightly rolled and separated by denomination as they were back when he and Odraye had counted the money in his garage.

"Hot-damn, motherfucker! Better be all there, too."

"You want me to count it?" Butchie asked him.

"Naw, that'll be my job. Where you want it, Butchie? A head shot quicker, but I'm thinking, but man, you put me to so much fuckin' trouble, I'm going to gonna have to give you one in the guts—watch you squirm around on the floor. See this?" Odraye pulled a roll of duct tape from his pocket. "This'll keep you from screaming too loud. Can't be waking the neighbors now, can we?"

The punch Odraye delivered to the left side of Butchie's face wasn't as hard as the one back in the Club's parking lot, but it took his legs out from under him and he hit the floor. The smell of cat urine wafted into his nostrils and a red mist startled to settle over his eyes. He was conscious, however, and able to fight the mental confusion, fortunate he was not blacking out. He'd feared the sudden, unannounced bullet, but this was worse; he had not anticipated the man's sadism.

Odraye finished wrapping Butchie's mouth. "Holler your

lungs out now, boy."

He dragged him by the shoulders to the refrigerator and propped him against the open door.

"Don't want the slug going through you and into that house back there," Odraye said.

He stepped back as if gauging the distance and angle.

He unloaded one bullet and replaced it with one from his pocket.

"This one's a Glaser safety round."

Butchie squeezed his eyes shut, waiting for it, warm urine wetting his crotch. . .

"You're going to feel it expanding in your guts and you won't—Who's there?"

Butchie didn't hear Odraye. His brain was already squirting some enzyme from the amygdala, preparing him for death, easing a little of the horrendous pain about to befall him.

Floorboards, boots, thumps.

I said who's there?

A shot.

Butchie covered his stomach instinctively. But he wasn't hit. He wasn't shot. It's not me, his brain yelled, it's not me—

A second shot. A grunt from somewhere in the other room. The sound of something large crashing to the floor.

Hoyt staggered into view, his hands fumbled with the flashlight. The beam played across his face like a miniature lighthouse beacon, sweeping the floor, probing into the darkness where Butchie sat, back to his face with its Cheshire grin coming undone.

Butchie watched the lower half of Hoyt approaching him but there was something wrong in the walk. It seemed to Butchie, slowly coming through the haze of his own near-death, to be that of a man trying to walk but finding it difficult.

Not the dark because he can't see, Butchie thought. He's been shot.

Hoyt staggered into the middle of the room and swept the flashlight beam into all the corners before settling it on Butchie, who was pulling off the duct tape and hunks of hair with it. A clunk, something metallic hit the floor. Hoyt bent down, searching the floor with his light until it shone on the steel baton, its scales fully extended.

"Hit him—hit him with this," Hoyt said.

He snapped his wrist and it retracted, a cobra strike. He slipped it into a loop of his vest.

"Where did he get you, Hoyt?"

"Flesh wound. . . God damn it, it hurts. But it's nothing," Hoyt said. "Lucky shot."

Butchie kept his eyes on Hoyt. His hand slipped down his pant leg. Hoyt's beam found him again and traced him with the beam as if he were trying to outline him in the darkness.

"You pissed yourself," Hoyt said.

"He was going to kill me."

Hoyt laughed.

"Why is that funny, Dominic?"

Hoyt stepped over to the bags. His legs wobbled, unsteady, like a drunk's.

"That it?"

His beam stabbed the bags. Butchie must have kicked one over. Dozens of banded bills were scattered across the floor. He stooped over and picked one up and turned it over in his hand.

"How much?"

"Two hundred, sixty-three thousand," Butchie said.

"Nice," Hoyt replied. He stuck the flashlight under his armpit and aimed the beam at the money as if he were cradling a baby chick.

Hoyt's voice, soft, reassuring. "You know what's next—"

Butchie aimed for the spot where the flashlight had been tucked: pop-pop-pop-pop-pop.

Hoyt wheeled toward him and swung the baton at his head guided by muzzle flash. The baton slammed into his shoulder breaking the clavicle.

Hoyt had Butchie by the throat and lifted him straight into the air and slammed him backwards into the fridge knocking all the air out of Butchie's lungs. He slumped to the floor, badly dazed.

"Not you! Not you! Not the likes of a piece of shit like you. . . Not possible. . ."

Hoyt's hoarse, wheezing breath came with a gurgle. Sucking chest wound. Butchie hadn't missed but he wasn't out of danger from the man. Hoyt's brute strength was diminishing by the second, time wasted looking for his weapons, a gun clattered to the floor, then he bulled into the fridge, slamming his feet into Butchie's hunched form. Butchie, semi-conscious, rolled to the side as Hoyt's steel-toed boot smashed in the fridge.

Butchie's groan gave him away. Hoyt staggered to him, reached down for his face and with claw-like fingers attempted to find his eyeballs.

"Take. . . you . . . with me. . . now."

It was like having acid splashed in Butchie's face. He twisted his head to get those talons out of his eye sockets.

The dark saved Butchie. He rolled to the other end of the wall before he passed out from the pain.

Butchie came to but how much time had passed, he didn't know. He was unable to rise to his feet because of the broken shoulder, bone grinding against bone. He vomited. When he was finally able to stand upright, he couldn't see anything. His right eye was swollen shut. Sweat or blood, probably both was dripping from his face to the floor.

Hoyt's flashlight lay ten feet from where he braced himself against the wall. He couldn't see Hoyt and he panicked. His Pico was gone. He headed for the flashlight on the floor. It seemed a long way off and it took an eternity to get there—a man dying of thirst crossing the Gobi.

He didn't know if he could bend down without falling but he had to chance it.

He reached for the light, a titanium number, and it felt good in his hand.

Hoyt was lying on his back with his eyes lidded, a slit of eyeball, but no pupil movement when Butchie shone the light straight into them. He looked peaceful. He flashed the light around and found his Beretta.

Sirens. About fucking time, Butchie thought.

He staggered into the next room and found Odraye. He was breathing, a thick, mucous-filled drawing of breath. Hoyt's baton had opened a huge wound in his scalp; the worm of blood that looked black until Butchie's light hit it traced a zig-zag path down the back of his hoodie, soaking it, and leaked onto the floor.

Butchie stood over him listening to the susurrus of breath followed by a catch—he's coming around.

Odraye's eyes opened and he snorted once.

"See me, Odraye?"

"Ugh," Odraye groaned.

"Good enough."

Butchie placed the gun at his temple and squeezed the trigger. The explosion was partially muted by the density of Odraye's head. The damage was terrific. No exit wound but it seemed that Odraye had acquired a head three times its original size as the expanding gases filled every space and bullet fragments tore and punched their way into his brain. It blew up like a small beach ball and then slowly deflated.

Not much time now, Butchie knew.

He returned to the room and picked up the loose wads of cash and stuffed them back inside the bag. He placed both bags back inside the refrigerator and then took the second padlock out of his pocket. He locked the handle to the side of the door with a large U-bolt he'd attached that day.

Now, then, what's left to do?

Butchie looked around the room. A shaft of moonbeam appeared in the gaping hole in the roof and swathed the filthy room with millions of tiny motes.

Butchie enjoyed the spectacle, oblivious to six members of Brockton's finest pouring through the door in SWAT gear, beams crisscrossed the front of the store, swaying from one corner to the other, until they found him. He was speckled with red laser dots. Someone screamed instructions at him to do something, but he realized he couldn't speak or understand

English anymore. When he fell to the floor in a heap, he took all the red dots with him.

CHAPTER 21

Butchie's eyes opened. The morphine drip was still there, thank God. But when he turned his head, there was the other fixture of his hospital room: Det. Sgt. Ray Forshey.

"Do you ever sleep?" Butchie asked him. "No family to go home to."

"I consider you my family, Butchie," Forshey replied.

"How long was I out this time?"

Forshey checked his wristwatch. "Not long, twenty minutes."

"Don't you ever get sick of vending-machine coffee?"

"What I get sick of, Mister Parmenter, is people lying to me all the time."

"I don't recall lying to you, exactly," Butchie said.

He fiddled with the remote to raise the bed. No matter which position, the discomfort remained the same. On the wall near Forshey's head was a pain chart for kids: a row of smiley faces that turned upside-down as the level of pain increased.

"It's what you haven't said," Forshey said, leaning back in his chair.

Sins of omission, Fr. Montesanti called those. . .

"Here's the thing—" Forshey began, leaning toward him with his fingers interlocked on his knees, his voice soft, lulling as always, even his damned phone messages.

He'd make a good priest, Butchie thought.

"We got two bodies on the floor, all the weapons, including that steel club gizmo. Ballistics is matching it up with the autopsy reports. So we're gonna know who shot who and who tried to whip the brains out of Odraye Suggs head, which, come to think of it, was a little overkill considering the head shot."

"Want to hear my theory?"

"No. Keep your theory, Butchie," Forshey said.

"OK."

"Odraye Suggs, we know all about. Got a record. Small-timer, sometime boxer, sometime scammer, petty thief, drug dealer—no arch criminal, in other words."

"How can you be so sure?"

"Shut up. But this—this Dominic Hoyt. Who is he? He's carrying a private investigator's license. He has no criminal record, not even a traffic ticket in the state of Massachusetts. He lives with his mother in a duplex in Waltham."

"Someone told me he was military, served in the Middle East," Butchie said.

"No, we checked. No military service. He's never been out of the country, never applied for a passport. Here's the weird thing—I mean, aside from the bullet holes drilled into him—he has no driver's license, no social security card, no work history we can find, no financial records. He's a ghost. He lives—lived—off the grid."

"I didn't think that was possible," Butchie said. He remembered Hoyt's words that day: This is America. You are who you say you are. . .

"We checked with the Bello family. John Bello says the family didn't hire him. His license is phony."

"When do you plan to arrest me?"

"Why?"

"When they brought me in here, I was handcuffed to the rails of the bed," Butchie replied.

"It's in discussion," Forshey said; "we're still investigating."

"I'm ready to make a statement right now," Butchie said.

"Pretty cocksure, aren't you?"

"That's an interesting word, Detective. We should keep it alive in our conversations, feminism be damned."

"I think the dope they're giving you is making you goofy,"

Forshey said.

Forshey was right about that. Butchie had trouble seeing out of the one eye and the skin around both eyes felt as if his face had been massaged with sandpaper.

"You cold? Want a blanket?"

"No, why?" Butchie asked.

"You shivered just now," Forshey replied.

"Just the meds," Butchie said. "Could be a problem for you if you arrest me now. My lawyer can say I was non compos mentis."

"Quite the lawyer, all of a sudden. Are you feeling guilty?"

"An altar boy. A long time ago," Butchie said.

"For what it's worth," Forshey said. "I'll take down whatever you want to say."

He pulled out a pocket recorder and set it on the bed next to Butchie's hand.

Butchie gave him the story in a bare-bones outline: he was lured to the Fratellanza Club by "an anonymous caller" who said his ex-girlfriend was there and wanted to talk about getting back together. Odraye Suggs attacked him in the parking lot and kidnapped him at gunpoint because he believed the rumor that Butchie had found Mrs. Bello's hidden money. He was forced at gunpoint to drive to the store. When no money was found, Suggs threatened to kill him. That's when Dominic Hoyt appeared.

Forshey grunted his disdain and stopped scribbling in his notebook.

"Really, Butchie? Just like that? He appears out of nowhere like a magician's rabbit?"

Butchie had no reply except to say Hoyt was after the money, too, and must have been following Suggs. "It was you who dropped me into this, Forshey. You named me in the paper. You dropped me right into the middle of it. You think that was the right thing to do?"

Butchie tried to feign indignation but Forshey wasn't buying it.

"Money has a scent of its own," he said. "It attracts

people."

"Tell me about it."

Forshey made Butchie repeat the last part of his story three times despite the recorder in the room.

"Suggs and Hoyt fight. It's dark, nobody can see that well. Hoyt uses the baton. You don't see it but you hear shots. Two loud booms in quick succession, then five shots not so loud. That it?"

"That's it, Detective. I was barely conscious at that time. Suggs hit me when I told him there was no money. I was just a housing inspector—"

"Yeah, yeah, blah-blah. Save it for another time, Butchie, because you're going to need it."

Butchie steadied his voice for the two-hundred-sixty-thousand-dollar question: "You found no money in the place, am I right?"

"Not exactly," Forshey said.

"What's that mean?"

"No hidden cache of money so far," he replied. "Some loose bills on the floor. Silver certificates, out of date. About two-hundred-sixty lying around that got trampled in the fight."

Butchie had stopped breathing.

Forshey looked at him. "Two hundred sixty-four dollars, to be exact."

"No money in the fridge, I take it?"

"No, why do you ask?"

"Just curious," Butchie said.

"We'll be there when they take the place down. Demolition's been postponed. John Bello wants to be there, he said. It was slated for the day after tomorrow, according to your former boss Asaro, who doesn't have much good to say about you, by the way."

"The old lady could have found a spot nobody's looked into," Butchie said, trying to be helpful but his heart pounded with joy: Forshey's forensics people didn't get it.

"Or it was never there in the first place," Forshey said. "We had bodies on the floor, remember? We had things to do."

At the doorway, Forshey put on his hat and tucked his notebook and recorder into pockets.

"Fancy fedora you got there, Forshey," Butchie said.

"My copper hat," he said. "Thinning hair. I need it. Say, Butchie one more question, if you don't mind. A small thing."

"Ask away, Detective."

"The night they brought you in here. You made a phone call around three in the morning."

"How do you know that?"

"You asked a night nurse if you could borrow her phone. Who'd you call? You made a damn big fuss, she said, until you got it. Broken scapula, one eye completely closed, half out of it from the beating you took."

"Honestly, I don't remember. I must have been out of it," Butchie said.

"That's all right," Forshey said. "We'll find out."

The hospital decreased the morphine drip and the pain increased proportionally over the next three days. No word from Bobby Steele, but he wasn't worried. Bobby would know not to call him. Butchie would attract too much attention if he tried to wander around the hospital with a mobile bag drip looking for a landline phone. The one at the end of the hall in the visitor room would wind up on the hospital phone records and he didn't want to draw too much attention to Bobby.

Two-hundred-sixty dollars, Forshey said that day he came for his statement. An omen or a coincidence? Butchie wasn't sure of anything anymore. Maybe they had the money all along and were waiting for me to trap myself with a damaging admission. The papers were going crazy with it. The nurses kept reporters from badgering him but that was on Forshey's instructions, they told him. He wasn't on ICU status, so they could have gotten to him in his room.

Messages, no doubt, were piling up on his cell phone every day but that was one of the first things they'd confiscated when they brought him in. His clothes were cut from him and bagged up. He wasn't so out of it he didn't notice the pair of latex gloves taking his things from the nurse. His condition kept them from doing a gunshot residue test on his hands, but they didn't need that if they had his clothes.

Still, no charges filed. He didn't care about any secret indictments. Butchie's plans accommodated that possibility with his new identity.

Dominic Hoyt gave him a lot to think about during daylight hours. Who was the guy? Just somebody who got a whiff of money and decided to follow the trail straight to Butchie? He felt some satisfaction in dropping him into his statement to the cop, let him serve me as my deus ex machina, Butchie thought. Old Sister Regis, a withered crone with a thousand wrinkles and a light film of dead skins cells powdering her face so that she always came into class looking as if she'd stepped offstage with pancake makeup on. She would have been proud of his use of the term from her seventh-grade English class.

He decided to chance it; the suspense was churning up his guts too much. He couldn't tolerate the hospital food. He waited for Bobby's shift to start, late afternoon.

"Hey, Bobby."

"Butchie, how's tricks?"

"Still in the hospital," Butchie said. "They're releasing me tomorrow. Thought I'd drop by then, say hello, and thank you for. . .your friendship."

"That's what friends are for, Butchie. You remember that time we came back from the Cathedral, both of us too shitfaced to drive and you said, "'Bobby, take the wheel. I trust you.'"

"I do. Boston won two against the Yanks," Butchie said.

"Remember when I hit ninety-five in that old heap of yours and shut off the lights?"

"I was shitting myself," Butchie said.

"But you didn't say a word the whole time. You trusted me, right?"

"Still do, Bobby."

"Hey, look, I gotta go. Customers lining up at the bar like camels at an oasis."

Thank you, Jesus. . . Thank you, Bobby.

Bobby would know about camels and oases. He served in Afghanistan with a forward combat engineers platoon. Saw his share of action. Knew how to blow things up and how to build things. Bobby told him, citing Army regs, a combat engineer's duty was to impede the enemy and facilitate movement and support of friendly troops.

Bobby Steele had no trouble crawling through a tenement lot in the middle of the night and extracting a quarter-million in bundles of money with his prosthetic hand while detectives and cops milled about a crime scene. Cops securing the area outside and Forshey's men inside busy conducting an onsite double homicide investigation while the blood was still pooling around the victims' heads. Too busy to crack open my padlock on the refrigerator door until five in the morning, or so Forshey had said. He'd called Bobby Steele at Bittaker's not a minute too late. Bobby drank for an hour after closing time and went home. Bobby had never told him or anyone where he lived in all the years he'd known him.

CHAPTER 22

One Month Later, Big Pink Key, FL

Butchie's nearest neighbor on his right was from Coeur D'Alene who sold heart stents. The one on the left of his double-wide was also a retiree. He was an actuarial statistician, he said, for a major insurance company, but that was all Butchie knew except for the fact they both were widowers, retired, in their mid-seventies. In fact, he reckoned ninety-percent of the people in his trailer park were retirees. He felt like a kid.

They all called him Tom, which was the name on the tab of his mailbox: Thomas Parmentieri. One widow with five or six cats who'd retired from a Fortune 500 company called him "Tommy" and brought him chocolate-chip cookies the day after he moved in.

He furnished the place on the cheap. One of the tenants had died intestate and the sale of his belongings provided all but the television, the Keurig, the dishes, and the dining room set. He'd even taken the man's book shelves and most of the books. He had no appetite for political memoirs, as the old fellow obviously had, but he had all his philosophy books, an extensive collection of old hardbacks from Aristotle's Poetics to Zoroastrianism. Butchie had already started at the end of the alphabet and read a little here and there, what he could comprehend which, he admitted, wasn't much but he hoped to get better. He was delighted with the idea of the world locked in an epic battle between good and evil. He thought that made sense, even though he knew Fr. Montesanti would not agree and would have said so through the veins in his neck. God does not compete with the devil for the soul of man!

Butchie wasn't so sure, not after what he'd experienced in the last few months. His wounds were healed up or healing nicely, even his vision was back to normal. Like most Florida natives (he considered himself one), he avoided the sun but for all his lotions and sun blocks, his skin was turning a healthy bronze and the peeling was mostly behind him. He'd gone paragliding, deep-sea fishing off Islamorada (bagged a marlin and a razor-toothed Wahoo); he bought himself a surf board at a shop in Key West. Life was good.

Big Pine was short on everything he had in Brockton—mainly cold weather, snow squalls, and traffic gridlock. No strip malls, shopping centers or megastores, crowds of people and traffic everywhere you went. Homeless people, scammers, the human sharks who preyed on the weak. Another thing: you didn't speed; all the signs were posted at 35 m.p.h. to protect the elusive Key deer. He'd yet to spot one and thought they were a myth like unicorns, but everyone said they existed. There was a skydiving club at Sugarloaf Key he intended to explore soon. He discovered he had no fear of heights at all. So far, he was happy to go fishing every other day, nap in the afternoons, and snorkel around Looe Key Marine Sanctuary. Living between the Gulf of Mexico to the north and the Atlantic Ocean to the south was bliss. Stepping out of his trailer at night to locate a few constellations, Butchie tracked Sirius, the Dog Star as his own lucky star. Butchie didn't think he could tire of it.

He'd spent little money so far and made no plans for the future except for side trips to Miami or down to Key West. He wanted to see Havana before New Year's. He left the Saturn behind in Homestead when it started blowing huge plumes of blue smoke and leaking transmission fluid. It was as if it got him to where he needed to be. He piled his cash on top of the second bed in the motel, went across the street to a flea market and bought used leather motorcycle saddlebags; that afternoon, he walked into the first bank in Homestead he saw. Wendy, the assistant manager, listened to his story of an eccentric aunt, a collector of bric-a-brac—"She loved Delft-Blue plates, especially, poor old thing"—but she was a notorious hoarder in the family. Butchie lifted the saddlebags. "Here's what she left me. I'd like to put it into an account at your bank."

She was so pretty, the opposite of Neecie's olive-complected skin and dark hair; a true blonde with translucent skin and blue eyes the color of sea ice. He'd stayed in Homestead while they had a three-week sexual affair that ended well for both. Butchie locked into his neocortex the image of her stepping out of her panties with that tawny swirl of pubic hair twisted like a flame.

His—rather, Tommaso Parmentieri's—social security, library card, and Massachusetts ID enabled him to open the bank account, which he divided between a savings and checking. One-hundred-five thousand apiece. Easy-peasy, done in ten minutes. Butchie walked into the Florida sunlight full of jasmine scents and thought FBI agents were going to descend on him any second.

He called Neecie one night after fortifying himself with some Scotch. The conversation was moving along fine, he thought, no tears or you-bastard accusations—that is, until she dropped the bomb: "I'm engaged."

"Do I know him?"

"No, somebody I met at work," she said.

"Kinda fast, Neecie."

"I'm getting old, Butchie. I can't stay single forever. My sister's oldest kid is turning eleven next week," she said.

Italian girls, Ma-drrone! The boys all said in high school. They mature so fast, sprout boobs you can see coming down the corridor, and then—AND THEN THEY TURN INTO THEIR MOTHERS! The guys sang the last part like a chorus.

He was about to hang up when she said, "That cop, what's-his-name?"

"Forshey," Butchie said. "Detective Forshey."

"Yeah, he keeps calling here asking if I've heard from you."

"What did you tell him?"

"Nothing," she said. "I told him you ain't called and I didn't expect you to."

The truth, he realized.

"Thanks for telling me," Butchie said. "So long, Neecie."

"Wait! He said, the cop said he was going to be in Key West this year. He says he goes on vacation down there every year. He said if I was to hear from you, I was to tell you where you could meet up with him—if you wanted to talk about. . . anything."

"My girl—my former girlfriend—told me you were going to be here," Butchie said.

Florio's was a nice bar, Butchie decided. Not too many tourists. Already he was thinking like a native. Forshey surprised him by showing up in Bermuda shorts, sandals, and a shirt with palm trees.

"Damn, these Mojitos are good," he told Butchie. "You think I would have had one of these before now."

"Somehow, I think you're lying to me," Butchie said.

"Honest to God," Forshey said. "How's your shoulder?"

"Healing nicely. So now we're here, and I don't see any US Marshals disguised in parrot shirts anywhere, what do you want with me?"

"Just thought we'd catch up, you know. Old times, that kind of thing."

"Come on, Forshey. Cut the shit," Butchie said. It took him a couple Mojitos to relax. He still half-expected to see those US Marshals.

"You're in the clear," Forshey said. "No indictments. Nolle prosequi, as they say in the Commonwealth Attorney's Office. You don't look happy."

"I am happy."

"I said you were free from prosecution, Butchie. I didn't say you were innocent. We're pretty sure you killed one or both of those men."

"How can you be sure?"

"Mathematics, logic. The bodies told us so. Trouble is, not

anything we can sell to a jury and those two—well, not to put too fine a point on it, juries don't really care when scumbags get street justice. One gangbanger kills another, who cares? It's beneficial population adjustment."

"I see."

"Do you? Your friend, the bartender at Bittaker's. He's been hocking a lot of silver certificates lately, putting bills on eBay. Getting twenty, twenty-five points over for dollar bills."

"Are you saying he stole Mrs. Bello's money?"

"No, Butchie. You stole that money."

Butchie didn't bother to deny it. Just then, some pretty girls came into the bar laughing and giggling. Bar-hopping, Butchie thought. Pretty young snowbirds. Maybe they all had dull secretarial jobs back home. Some of them left boyfriends or husbands and dirty diapers behind to cut loose in the sun for a couple weeks, dining in restaurants serving conch salad and clubbing in bars with coconuts stuck in palm fronds in the rafters would help to convince you life could be different, better. He thought of Neecie again.

"I don't know what you mean, Detective."

"Look, Butchie, I can't arrest you. I want to, Lord knows. But I can't. The DA up there says the case won't fly. It doesn't hurt you that everybody else involved is dead."

"Keep at it, Forshey, as I'm sure you will. Maybe someday—who knows?—you'll make a case."

"I don't think so, Butchie—oh, sorry, Thomas, I meant. You go by Tom or Tommy down here?"

"Either is fine," Butchie said.

"I'm not wasting my time on identity fraud, in case you were worried. Be whoever you are."

"Yet here you are, Forshey," Butchie said.

"Yes, here I am. I just might retire down here. But I think I'd miss the North, even the cold, the way people talk. It's home. Here, everybody's acting like they're at a carnival. It's not. . . real."

"Real enough for me," Butchie replied.

"You ever hear of a dead cat bounce?"

"Nope, never did. Sounds like some kind of anti-Audubon activity."

"No, no, no. It's got nothing to do with real cats or even dead cats," Forshey said. "I heard it the other day before I left for the Keys. Two hotshot attorneys from the DA's were in the precinct talking in the elevator. They were talking about stocks, investments. One of them said to the other about some stock he bought that just went up ten points. The other guy said, "That's a dead cat bounce, Manny. That stock will crash soon."

"And your point, Detective?"

"I guess. . . I guess my point is this. Something that seems too good to be true is too good to be true, Butchie. Think about it."

"So long, Forshey."

Butchie finished his drink and set a couple twenties on the bar. Seeing Forshey's gaze follow the bills to the counter top, he smiled.

"I got those at the bank around the corner an hour ago," Butchie said.

"Cheers, Butchie. . . Thomas, whatever."

"Goodbye, Forshey. You're . . . you're all right," Butchie said.

Butchie stood aside while a young couple came inside the bar. Their happiness was so transparent, he felt a pang of anguish.

"Butchie," Forshey called out to him from his stool.

The cop was a little drunk, Butchie realized as soon as he'd taken the stool beside him. The New England detective looked downright ridiculous, the stereotypical snowbird—pale, sunburnt skin, freckled hands, thinning hair approaching combover stage, skinny shanks, and that ridiculous shirt. But Butchie envied him nonetheless. He could go home.

"What, Forshey?"

"You change your mind—you know, about making things right so you can sleep?—just FedEx me the money in a box."

"Maybe I'll put it in saddlebags and loop it over Rocky

Marciano's right arm in Champions Park," Butchie said.

Forshey's laugh was a series of high-pitched yips, a coyote chorus.

"Just call me first so I can get it to the Bellos," he said. "Let them fight over it," he said.

"I'll think about it," Butchie said.

He walked out into the sunshine of another gorgeous day in the Keys. Butchie decided to walk down to Sunset Pier to see if that famous green flash happened when the sun disappeared in an emerald wink on the horizon's edge. It was enough to make a man philosophical about life.

THE END

About the author

Robb White is the author of two hardboiled private-eye novels featuring his existentialist detective Thomas Haftmann, both published by Grand Mal Press: Haftmann's Rules (2011) and Saraband for a Runaway (2013). His crime novel Special Collections was the winner of the 2014 Electronic Book Series Competition by New Rivers Press. "Frotteur in the Dark" was selected by 10,000 Tons of Black Ink as one of 6 Best Of for 2009. That story was published in the collection "Out of Breath" and Other Stories by Red Giant Press of Cleveland in 2013. White also writes book reviews and does interviews for Tom Huff's magazine Boxing World.

Also by the same author

Northtown Eclipse (Volume 1: Raimo Jarvi Investigates)

Northtown Blitz (Volume 2: Raimo Jarvi Investigates)

When You Run With Wolves

Printed in Great Britain
by Amazon

52411256R00101